A ROLE TO DIE FOR

THE COFFEE HOUSE SLEUTHS
BOOK 3

T. LOCKHAVEN

EDITED BY:
GRACE LOCKHAVEN

TWISTED KEY
publishing

2025

First Printing: 2025

ISBN 978-1-63911-185-5

Twisted Key Publishing, LLC
www.twistedkeypublishing.com

Ordering Information:
Special discounts are available on quantity purchases by corporations, associations, educators, and others. For details, contact the publisher at the above listed address.

Contents

Chapter 1

"Who reads this drivel? It's utterly atrocious."

Temperance Austin tossed Jessica North's new romance thriller onto her nightstand. With a huff, she threw her head backward onto a mountain of pillows, her hair spilling over her shoulders.

Brett Angel, her fiancé, closed his eyes and waited. The anticipation of knowing this was just a precursor of what was yet to come was unnerving.

"Love!" she finally gasped, her eyes flying open impossibly wide, her chest heaving.

Even though Brett knew the outburst was inevitable, he still jumped when she shouted.

"Every romance book treats love like a *formula*. Like you're baking a cake. Follow these *simple* steps, add these *simple* ingredients," she said mockingly, "and you'll find *true* love and happiness. I'm *highly* offended by the author's sheer audacity. Remind me to leave a *scathing* review for her *book* tomorrow," Temperance fumed.

Brett drew in a long, slow breath. "I will," he promised.

She gave him a tortured look, as if she doubted his commitment to her cause.

"I *will*," he exclaimed more forcefully. "Now get some sleep; we've got a big day tomorrow." He gently kissed her forehead and reached for the lamp when she began ranting again.

"Jessica North knows *nothing* of the nuances of love. Love is *not* a cake, Brett. Do you think love is a cake?"

Before he could answer, Temperance leapt from the bed, dragging the blankets with her, leaving Brett stretched out in his boxers and socks, like a body on a gurney.

"Never mind! I need closure. I must do it tonight or I won't be able to sleep." She marched across the room, grabbed her laptop from her dresser, and flung it onto the bed. It landed with a *thud* beside Brett. She plopped back down beside him and retrieved the laptop—rested it on her outstretched legs and flipped it open.

"This literary travesty *must* be dealt with."

Brett drew in a long, deep breath, filling his lungs. He turned an anguished face toward the camera and exhaled. "It's going to be a long, long night."

"And cut!" called out a commanding voice. A bell rang, and instantly, the movie set was filled with activity.

Victoria Day swung her long legs over the side of the bed, crossed the bedroom, and stopped in front of the full-length mirror attached to a closet door. A woman in a frumpy flannel shirt and blue jeans rushed over, placing a silk robe over the actress's shoulders.

"You were amazing, Ms. Day," the woman gushed. The starlet ignored her, waving off her comment with a flick of her hand, like she was flicking ash from a cigarette. The assistant scurried away; she knew her place.

Victoria ignored the crew gathered behind her. She tilted her head and narrowed her eyes. A wicked smile crossed her lips. She'd seduced many a man with those eyes: producers, directors, sports stars, millionaires, and billionaires. But as she drew closer, she didn't like what she saw. Hollywood wasn't kind to aging actors, especially women—unless you were Meryl Streep; she could do no wrong. Only a few choice women continued to be considered Hollywood royalty.

A flicker of fear and self-doubt briefly fluttered inside her. Beneath her expertly made-up face, she could see small, thin lines spidering out from the corners of her eyes. Her once luscious brown hair, now dry and lifeless, rested on her tan shoulders.

Her finger touched the puffy skin beneath her eyes—too much drinking and too little sleep. She should have felt guilty showing up to set like this, but… she chased the foolish thought away. *They can take care of that in post-production.* Victoria turned from the mirror; what she needed right now was a cigarette and her stylist.

Ian Stewart—the actor who played her fiancé Brett—rolled off the bed, hopped to his feet, and ran his fingers through his mess of curly brown hair. He made eye contact with his stylist just as she rolled her eyes. He gave her an embarrassed smile and mouthed, "Sorry."

"Ian," his stylist chided him, "what am I going to do with you?"

Ian was prone to nervous habits. She'd broken his nail-biting stint, his neck-rubbing habit, and now she had a new one to address. She fussed with his hair a bit and touched up his makeup. A woman handed Ian a robe, which unlike Victoria, he graciously accepted. Ian shrugged it on, thanking her.

He slid his feet into a pair of slippers and padded over to the video village, where he joined Noah Cruise, the cinematographer, and David Brooke, the director, to watch the playback of the scene.

David Brooke shook his head and removed his headphones. "I think we need to tone down Victoria's reaction to the book a little."

Ian met David's eyes and nodded. "Just a tad," he agreed.

"And we need another light, over by the doorway," added Noah. "There's too much shadow on Victoria's face."

"Did I hear my name?" Victoria crossed the set to where the men were huddled around the monitor.

"Yes," David replied. He removed his baseball cap and scratched his closely cropped salt-and-pepper hair. "Noah was suggesting a change in lighting. There's a bit too much shadow on your face when you turn toward Ian in the shot."

"Thank you, Noah." Victoria rubbed his arm. "You're always looking out for me."

"And…" David continued cautiously, "the reaction to the book was splendid," he paused for a beat.

"I know," Victoria snipped, "*exactly* what you were looking for."

David sighed. "Not quite. We're almost there," he quickly added. "How about we try taking it down, just a tad bit?"

"Take it down? I *know* you're not accusing me of *overacting*, David!" Victoria exclaimed coldly.

The set fell quiet behind them. The crew had been warned not to react—Victoria thrived on nothing more than a captive audience.

"Victoria," David replied calmly, trying to keep things from escalating. "We're going to fall way behind schedule if you continue to second-guess me every time I ask to reshoot a scene."

Victoria's jaw tightened, and she inhaled sharply. "Well, Noah did say that there was too much shadow on my face."

"Yes, he did," Ian said softly. He put his arm around her shoulders, in an effort to defuse the intensity of the moment. "We've got this. Let's do the reshoot. I was a little off on my timing, anyways."

"And perhaps, a little less drinking," David mumbled, a little too loudly.

Victoria stopped in her tracks and wheeled on David, her face darkening. "I thought you *liked it* when I drank," she hissed.

Ian cut his eyes at David, *unbelievable*. He couldn't stop himself. "I'm going to need five," said Ian, shaking his head.

"No!" Victoria grabbed Ian's hand and pulled him toward the bed. "Come on; David doesn't like *drama* in the bedroom, unless he's involved." She turned and gave him a withering look.

Chapter 2

It was a cold, dreary December morning in the quaint coastal town of Lana Cove, North Carolina. The sky was pencil-led gray. The air was heavy, filled with moisture. Nasty weather was on its way.

Ellie Banks eased her sleek black rental van to a stop in front of a large wrought-iron gate that protected the private drive of the Marlow Estate, owned by investment banker, philanthropist, Evan Marlow.

A young man dressed in a wool overcoat, stocking cap, and red scarf emerged from a small wooden structure that resembled a fancy outhouse. He hurried over to the driver's side door with the grace of a surefooted mountain goat. Ellie lowered the window and smiled down at the pink-faced man. "Good morning."

"Morning, ma'am." The gate attendant wiped at his bright red nose with his sleeve; a tuft of brown hair had escaped his stocking cap and curled into a small *c* on his forehead. "May I help you?"

"I'm Ellie Banks from Bitter Sweet Café."

"Craft services." The young man nodded.

"Yes," said Ellie. She leaned back in her seat and gestured to her right. "And this is my assistant Michael West."

"Morning." Michael leaned forward and waved. "Liam," he said, reading the attendant's name badge. "How do you like your coffee?"

Liam wrinkled his brow quizzically for a moment, and then realized Michael was serious. "That won't be necessary, sir, thank you."

"Nonsense," Michael insisted. "I have everything right here." He gestured to a series of metal canisters and a hotbox on the floor between his feet.

"I don't know"—Liam shrugged—"a smidgen of cream with two sugars, I guess."

"Coming right up." Michael rested the cup on the console and then busied himself, preparing Liam's coffee from a large silver canister.

The man swiped his gloved finger across his tablet and scrolled. "Give me just a moment, please, Miss Banks." He continued swiping downward and then stopped. "Here you are, Bitter Sweet Café. Ellie Banks and Michael West."

"That's us," Ellie replied.

"If you could just use your finger and sign *here*, please." Liam passed the tablet to Ellie. She signed it and returned it to him.

"Orders up," Michael piped cheerfully. He handed the coffee and a bagel wrapped in aluminum foil to Ellie.

"Coffee and a bagel with cream cheese." Ellie smiled, passing him the beverage and food through the window.

"A bagel too?" The young man shook his head as if it was the most incredible thing that had ever happened to him. "Fantastic! Thank you so much."

"You're welcome." Ellie laughed at the man's unabashed joy of an unexpected breakfast.

"Is this your first time to the Marlow Estate?" asked Liam.

"Yes," Ellie replied.

"Wonderful." Liam took a step back from her door. "Follow the drive until you arrive at the fork. Keep to the right; it will take you to the rear of the compound. Once you're there, Gerald from security will direct you where to go and provide you with IDs."

"Thank you, Liam." Ellie smiled. She raised the window and shifted into drive. The gate attendant stepped back and held up his coffee in a gesture of thanks as they passed by.

"Horrible job," Michael commented, shaking his head. "Especially in this weather. You couldn't pay me enough."

"Says the man who's helping me for free." Ellie shivered and jabbed at the button on the dash, increasing the heat. "I miss my seat warmers," she groaned.

Michael rubbed his hands together and offered them to Ellie, smiling mischievously.

"Ah, *too* late as usual." Ellie sighed. "We're already here."

Chapter 3

A security guard—dressed in an oversized bulky blue jacket that looked as if it had eaten another bulky blue jacket—held up a gloved hand and motioned for Ellie to stop. The word Security was plastered across the front of his black stocking cap. A wire from an earpiece coiled down his neck and disappeared beneath the collar of his coat. He edged around the front of the van and approached Ellie's window.

"Morning, Ms. Banks."

The security guard's face was raw, his lips cracked and red from the unrelenting wind coming off the ocean. Bits of sand and snow swirled around the van forming a mini cyclone.

"Yes, sir, from the Bitter Sweet Café."

The guard pulled a glove off with his teeth and reached into his jacket pocket. Ellie noticed the name Gerald embroidered on his jacket. His face and mannerisms reminded her of John Candy. A grumpy John Candy. He handed Ellie two identification badges.

"Clip them to a piece of clothing where they will *always* be visible," he said gruffly.

Ellie nodded, twisted in her seat and handed Michael his badge.

"This is amazing," Michael exclaimed, admiring the craft services badge. "I've always wanted one of these."

Gerald rolled his eyes, as if to say *another one*.

"You'll need to wear them whenever you're on set. If you lose your badge, you'll need to call security immediately so a new badge can be issued. You will *not* be allowed on set without your badge."

"Thank you, Gerald, we'll do our best to make sure that doesn't happen." Ellie gave him a big smile, which he didn't return. *He's probably heard that a million times*, Ellie thought.

A gust of wind stormed across the parking lot, Gerald tucked his chin against the steady buffeting.

"Unlock the back of your van, please, Ms. Banks. I have to make sure it's just you two."

"He's afraid we're smuggling in the Keebler Elves," Michael whispered.

"No problem," said Ellie, ignoring Michael. She pressed a button below the steering wheel. There was a metallic *thud* as the doors unlocked.

"I can't take a bad picture, can I?" Michael held up his ID badge for Ellie to see. Ellie closed her eyes; it was going to be a long day.

The back doors swung open, and then seconds later, slammed shut with a boom. Gerald returned and tapped on Ellie's window.

"Park over there, Ms. Banks—behind that white line so you can unload."

He pointed to the pavement that ended at two towering glass doors. Wreaths the size of car tires swung from side to side, their felt ribbons flapping and twisting in the wind.

"You'll be setting up inside the Dagmeyer suite."

Gerald slapped the side of the van like a cowboy in a westerner, and then stepped aside.

"Okay." Ellie nodded, amused by Gerald's antics. She waited until the window was up and then added, "He's a bit peculiar."

"He's got a unique personality," Michael agreed. "And that's saying something, coming from me."

Ellie cut the wheel to the left and pulled forward, stopping a few inches from the white line.

"Speaking of unique personalities"—she turned to Michael, giving him a playful smile— "I don't need to ask you to be on your best behavior, do I?"

Michael looked indignant. "Me?" He puffed up his chest. "You forget I was an award-winning executive at a prestigious firm in Boston. Etiquette and social grace are *synonymous* with the name *West*."

"So is the word *wild*," deadpanned Ellie.

She gathered her purse, grabbed the door latch, and slid out of the van.

"Ah!" She was startled—nose to nose with Gerald. She stumbled back a step. "I wasn't expecting you to be *right* behind me."

"*Always* expect the unexpected." Gerald arched a self-congratulatory eyebrow, clearly proud of his prowess. "It's why I'm good at my job."

Ellie shot a quizzical look at Michael. He shrugged, his expression saying, *What can I tell you—he's good at his job.*

"This way, Ms. Banks."

Gerald tugged open one of the behemoth glass doors. A rush of warm air filled with hints of cinnamon spilled out, wrapping around Michael and Ellie as they stepped inside. Classical holiday music filled the spacious room.

"Please remove your boots and place them on the drying rack." Gerald motioned to an Alpine wall-mounted boot and glove dryer. "You'll wear the Sure-Grip indoor shoes whenever you're in the mansion."

"They'll clash with my apron," Michael protested.

"You see that rug over there? It's a Savonnerie—worth nearly a million dollars."

"A million dollars?" Michael looked genuinely shocked. "You know," he said, inspecting his laceless Sure-Grip sneakers. "I think these shoes will accessorize perfectly with my apron."

"I thought so," Gerald grumbled. He strode forward—using his arms like the prow of a boat to part Michael and Ellie—took two steps, and then spun on his heels, raising a commanding hand. "This is the Dagmeyer Room." His eyes swept across the grandeur. "Anywhere you see blue tape, do not cross it. Understood?"

"Understood." Ellie and Michael nodded.

"You'll be setting up beneath the Cézanne."

He pointed to a spot about twenty feet away. There were two long tables set up end to end, cloaked in deep green tablecloths. A red felt rope cordoned the area off from the rest of the room.

"Perfect," Ellie said, eyeing the space, "I'm a big fan of Cézanne."

"Wonderful. An admirer of art," Gerald replied. He eyed Michael as if expecting a response.

"Sorry, I only follow the great masters of paint by numbers," said Michael with mock seriousness. "Hasbro, Mattel… and of course the immortal Crayola." Gerald's eyes narrowed into a flat dubious stare. "I see, not a fan," Michael muttered.

"I'll be back in twenty for coffee." Gerald tapped his watch. "Black." He spun on his heel to leave, then paused, muttering. "Almost forgot." He dug in his pocket, fished out a candy cane, and handed it to Ellie.

"Awe, thank you, Gerald," Ellie said with a smile.

Gerald's cheeks reddened. He reached in his pocket, lips pursed, fumbling until he came up with another. He smiled as he handed Michael a badly broken candy cane—the end suspiciously smooth, as if someone had already tested it.

"Eh… thank you, Gerald," said Michael, eyeing the slightly used candy cane.

Gerald grunted something unintelligible, spun on his heel again, and marched to the door. Without another word, he stepped out into the bitter cold.

"What an *odd* man," Ellie exclaimed.

"At least you two bonded over Cézanne."

Michael watched Gerald through the floor-to-ceiling windows as he struggled against the wind. He nodded as he passed two workers who were shoveling salt out of buckets, covering the walkways.

"Let's just make sure Gerald's coffee is ready in twenty minutes. I don't want to get on his bad side."

Michael nodded and breathed in deeply through his nose. He held up a gloved finger and sniffed a couple more times. "Cinnamon… vanilla… with a hint of elderberry. I must say, the rich smell *exquisite*."

"Gerald called it the Dagmeyer *Room*," said Ellie. "It's more like a *cathedral*."

She ventured over to the Cézanne painting, inspecting the roped-off space. Directly behind it, towering windows stretched across the wall, offering a spectacular view of the ocean. A set of lighted steps descended from a white stone terrace to a covered pier that jutted into the water like a wooden tongue.

Michael pointed to a strip of beach just beyond the pier, where an expensive-looking trailer squatted on the shoreline, its window glowing orange in the distance. "I wonder who's staying in the trailer."

"No idea." Ellie shrugged. "Whoever it is, they've certainly got a beautiful view."

"And a long walk to the house," Michael added. "We've got ice falling." He shook his head. "It's going to get nasty out there."

"You're right." Ellie nodded. "We better unload."

Chapter 4

Michael joined Ellie by the fireplace. He turned back toward the room, taking in marble statues of warriors armed with spears and swords, and goddesses who stood regally in every corner.

"Honestly, it's like a museum in here," he mused. "Who needs this much space?"

"Someone who has a *lot* of friends and does a lot of entertaining," Ellie replied.

"I suppose," Michael agreed. "Though I find his taste in sculptures *garish*," he said with an upturned nose.

Ellie's gaze slid over to the muscular nude in repose, lounging next to the Italian stone fireplace. "What's the matter, Michael, feeling a bit emasculated?" she teased.

"Please." Michael waved her comment aside. "Clearly it was cold the day that statue was carved."

Ellie chuckled. "A bit defensive, are we?" She smiled at him, then softened. "In all seriousness, thank you so much for offering to help." She touched his shoulder lightly. "I feel like you're always stepping in."

"Are you kidding? You couldn't have kept me away!" He flashed a boyish grin. "I'm *on* a movie set. It's Christmas… and I'm helping a friend. What more could a man ask for?"

"Good save." Ellie winked.

"I've got to say"—Michael let his eyes wander around the room—"I've wanted to do this since I was a kid."

"*Way* before I was born," Ellie teased, bumping his shoulder.

"Hey." Michael gave her a wounded look. "I'm not *that* much older than you."

"Tread lightly, mister," Ellie warned, giving him the evil eye.

Michael smiled. "It's just hard to believe that beyond those doors"—he gestured to a set of tall wooden doors across the room—"they're filming a movie. And, because of *you*, we're literally in the *same* house as some of Hollywood's biggest stars."

"It is a bit surreal," Ellie agreed, letting the moment sink in. Her phone buzzed, breaking the spell. A text from Olivia—her best friend and the other half of the Bitter Sweet Café.

Almost two years ago, Olivia and Ellie purchased a weathered bait-and-tackle shop and transformed it into the café. The residents of Lana Cove, a small, picturesque seaside town in

North Carolina, embraced the new owners, making their business a roaring success.

Unlike Ellie, Michael wasn't a Lana Cove native; he'd lived in Boston most of his life. He came to the seaside village after a bitter divorce and exhaustion from a thankless job. When his daughter left for college, he left too—Boston, his old job, his old self. What he wanted now was simple: to slow down, to write, to live.

Michael met Ellie and Olivia at the Bitter Sweet Café. They accepted him, warts and all, and helped him adjust to the unique lifestyle Lana Cove offered. Michael found his second home on their weather-worn deck, where he would write for hours. His friendship with Olivia had grown, but Ellie—she was the puzzle he could never quite solve.

Some pieces were slowly fitting together. Other pieces appeared unexpectedly. But many pieces were still missing, perhaps they hadn't even been created yet—or maybe Ellie had put them away, and she couldn't remember where. Michael wasn't in a hurry. Each new discovery made him realize how much she meant to him.

"I've always wanted to meet Ian Stewart," Ellie said casually, slipping her phone into her coat pocket.

"Who?" Michael replied, interrupted from his thoughts.

"Ian Stewart," Ellie repeated. "He seems so sweet. I hope that he's kind and magnanimous like his onscreen persona, and not a spoiled brat."

"Oh. I'm sure he's just *awful*," teased Michael. "Plus, I've heard from a reputable source that he turns into a *real* bear if he doesn't get his coffee first thing in the morning."

"Well, we can't have that!" Ellie declared. She eyed the doors that separated the two worlds. "I feel reasonably thawed." She smiled. "We best get everything set up."

Chapter 5

Ellie set to work brewing the coffee and setting up appliances: a toaster oven, a microwave. *Gerald must have gotten caught up with something*, Ellie thought. She hadn't seen him outside and he hadn't returned for his coffee.

Michael busied himself setting out pastries, cereal, fresh fruit, and breakfast sandwiches. He unboxed a brand-new six-slot toaster and plugged it in. A digital display appeared, showcasing choices for the type of toast you desired. "This thing has more settings than—"

"Brilliant! Coffee," said a tall woman with a clipped British accent. Her voice echoed throughout the cavernous room.

"Well, that's still up in the air," said Michael, brushing the wrinkles out of his *Bakers gonna bake* apron. "Our coffee's intellectual acumen has yet to be determined."

"Ha." The woman's eyebrows arched. "Aren't we the clever one? Been saving that one up, have we?"

"Well, I—"

The woman waved his reply aside. "I appreciate humor—however juvenile it may be," she added sardonically.

The woman wrapped her arms around a stylish oxblood leather jacket, cinched around her slender waist by a matching belt. Her auburn hair framed a squarish face, but it was her extraordinary hazel eyes that made her stand out from being just another pretty face.

"If I don't get Victoria her coffee soon…" She shuddered at the thought.

"Victoria Day," Michael gushed. "Hollywood's number one bad girl is here?"

"In the flesh, and she's demanding a double espresso caramel macchiato."

"I'll get that right away. Is that with soy, almond, low-fat milk?" Ellie inquired.

The woman lowered her eyes, meeting Ellie's. "She's seven stones soaking wet, darling, what do you think?"

"Seven stones?" Ellie looked to Michael for some guidance. "Is that some kind of new diet?"

"I think stones is a unit of measurement, if I'm not mistaken. I'll admit, it's a little confusing." Michael agreed. "Our friends across the pond use *stones* for weight and *pounds* for money. Go figure."

Ellie gave Michael a look and shook her head. "So, I'm still confused as to how Victoria would like her macchiato."

"I'd use low-fat to be on the safe side," Michael recommended.

The assistant nodded in agreement. "She's off her soy kick; she finds it too calming."

"Wouldn't want that." Michael nodded. "And you Miss—"

"Ashley, darling. No Miss, no Mrs." She jabbed at her phone again and then slipped it into her jacket pocket. "The formalities are unnecessary and simply make me feel *old*."

Michael noticed she eyed him conspicuously when she said the word *old*. She grabbed a cardboard to-go box and began scooping grapes and blueberries into it. "Also, I'll have an Americano, thank you."

"Certainly," Ellie replied over her shoulder.

Ashley closed the box and grabbed a set of plastic cutlery, *tsking* aloud. "Interesting. Still using plastic I see," she said, pulling a face. "Perhaps Bitter Sweet Café should invest in biodegradable utensils. I mean the ocean is *literally* right behind you." She gestured toward the windows.

"You're so right." Ellie smiled through her annoyance. "My apologies."

"If you have a moment, I could whittle something for you," Michael offered, pulling a pencil from his pocket. Ellie shot a warning glance his way.

Ashley rolled her eyes and let out an exaggerated sigh, "You're exasperating."

"Since we're on set," Michael spoke loud enough for both women to hear, "I was thinking—"

"*Out loud*, unfortunately," Ashley muttered, fishing her phone out of her pocket again.

Michael ignored her offhand comment and continued.

"I think we should change the names of our delicious beverages, you know, so they reflect our love of the movie-making industry."

He paused a beat, surprised neither woman seemed interested in participating in the nomenclature of morning beverages.

"Instead of your basic cappuccino, we could have the *Al Cappuccino*. Our delicious macchiato could pay homage to that classic cult favorite *The Karate Kid* with a Ralph Macchiato. You know, coffee with a kick." Michael attempted an ill-fated kick, grimaced, and clutched his hamstring.

"Oh my," Ashley murmured.

Ellie sighed loudly as she frothed the milk. "God help me, this is going to be a long day." Ashley looked at her and nodded sympathetically.

"So, if I may," Michael asked as he refilled the blueberries, "what's this movie about?"

"It's a Christmas romance," Ashley explained. "An exclusive bed and breakfast for the rich"—she opened her arms as if embracing the entirety of the mansion—"who are sharing Christmas together with a contest winner—an ordinary Joe writing his first novel—and his lovely fiancée."

"I'm guessing there is a lot of disdain," said Michael.

"Yes, the poor man is looked down upon by the others… but there is a twist at the end which is most gratifying. If you like that sort of thing."

"Oh, I love twists," said Ellie, pushing the two drinks into a cardboard carrier.

"Well, dot your calendars for next Christmas." Ashley smiled, scooping up the tray.

"Definitely," said Michael.

If Ashley heard him, she didn't respond. Michael watched enviously as she strode across the room, opened the door, and stepped into the magical world of movie-making.

Ellie glanced at her watch. In a few minutes there would be a hungry stampede of cast and crew. She quickly did another once-over. Everything was in order; she was ready; Michael was questionable.

Chapter 6

The light peppering of freezing rain against the windows had grown into a full-fledged ice storm.

A young man in a Bluey hoodie and Doc Martens hurried toward Peter Star and whispered in his ear. Peter nodded grimly, and the young man hurried off.

Peter closed his eyes, bracing himself. He was about to be the bearer of bad news. The sleigh ride shot had been delayed twice because of weather. He approached David cautiously, who was still seething after his row with Victoria.

"We've got an ice storm," said Peter. "Looks like it could last several—"

David slid his headphones down around his neck, his jaw tightening. "Alright." He nodded, his finger tapping the monitor. "Forget the sleigh scene. We're moving inside. Set up the Christmas dinner in the Dagmeyer Room."

"Got it." Peter nodded. He unclipped his walkie-talkie and began alerting the department heads to the change in plans.

"We just finished prepping the horses for the sleigh scene," a voice crackled back.

David snatched the walkie-talkie from Peter's hand. His voice snapped like a whip. "I'm not losing a day over freezing rain. We're shooting the dinner scene."

"Of course, David," the voice stuttered.

David handed the walkie-talkie back to Peter and was about to slip his headphones back on when Ian and Victoria joined them at video village.

"Did I hear Christmas dinner?" asked Victoria.

Peter shot Noah a look. Neither wanted any part of this. They both hurried off toward the Dagmeyer Room before the situation escalated.

In the distance, they could hear Victoria's voice raise. "I *just* got the rewrite last night!"

Chapter 7

The massive wooden doors separating the Dagmeyer Room from the rest of the house swung open. A crewman knelt and secured them so they would stay open.

"The portal has been opened," whispered Michael. He imagined rays of light blending with angelic voices pouring through into the Dagmeyer Room.

A team of men and women entered, pushing carts and dollies to the far corner of the room. Peter and Noah, walkie-talkies in hand, followed them.

Peter separated from the group and headed toward Ellie and Michael. "Good morning." He smiled.

"Good morning," Michael and Ellie replied in unison.

"I'm Peter Star," he continued, "AAD on this lovely production." He held out his hand.

"I'm Ellie Banks." She leaned over the table and shook his hand. "Nice to meet you."

Her eyes did a quick sweep of the man: blue eyes, strong jaw; she guessed he was in his later thirties—there was a hint of gray in his sideburns, and his stylish short brown hair was beginning to recede at his temples. He had a kind face and a pleasantness about him that Ellie imagined had a calming effect on others.

"And I'm Michael, her esteemed colleague," he said, breaking her trance.

"I'm sorry." Ellie blushed. "This is my first *on-set* catering gig—you mentioned you're an AAD?"

"Additional Assistant Director. Because you can never have too many directors." He chuckled at his own little joke.

Ellie laughed politely. She was quite sure he'd used that line dozens of times before. "So, you help the assistant director, who helps the director."

"Exactly." Peter nodded.

"I'm sure there's a *lot* to keep track of," Ellie offered, showing her respect for the importance of his position.

"More than you can imagine." He gave a knowing smile. "I'm so busy I have to wear two Fitbits."

"That is busy." Ellie laughed.

"So." Peter clasped his hands together. "As you've probably noticed, we'll be shooting at the far end of the room today. Since you're going to be in close proximity to the shoot, you'll need to be aware of some very specific rules you'll need to follow—we don't want to infuriate David."

"David's the director," Michael whispered to Ellie.

"First," Peter continued, "no phones or electronic devices that make noises. We can't have any *bips* or *beeps* going off during filming."

Michael and Ellie nodded as he spoke.

"When you hear 'quiet, please!' that's exactly what it means. When you hear the word 'rolling!', that means sound and camera are running. Stop what you're doing and stand still. Wait for the director to call 'cut!' or the buzzer to sound, which signals we are no longer rolling." Peter gave a reassuring smile. "Follow those rules and you'll do just fine."

"Not a problem, sir," Ellie replied, "we'll be as quiet as church mice."

"As long as they're not Pentecostal church mice." Peter chuckled at his own joke. "Oh, and one other piece of business."

Peter reached inside his jacket and retrieved a couple sheets of paper stapled at the top and a pair of red-framed reading glasses. He handed the papers to Ellie.

"What's this?" Ellie asked, skimming the page. Michael leaned over her shoulder, reading along.

"It's a call sheet," Peter explained. "Every day, members of the cast and crew receive a copy. If there are changes, we'll email you the night before. In a nutshell, it tells everyone when and where they are expected to be and what will be shot that day. I've taken the liberty of highlighting the times you'll be expected to be here and fully operational."

"Thank you." Ellie gave a firm nod. "I'll make sure that *everything* is set up and ready to go on time."

An appreciative smile traveled from Peter's mouth to his eyes.

"Thank you, Ellie. It's also important to check the call sheet the night before and the morning of. I can *promise* you they'll change."

He gestured to the corner of the Dagmeyer Room, now crawling with crew members.

"We were supposed to be shooting the winter sleigh ride scene today, but the weather had other ideas. It's just the nature of the beast. So, you'll need to be on top of things, and flexible."

"That won't be a problem." Ellie smiled reassuringly.

"If *anything*, Ellie is flexible." Michael smiled.

Ellie shot Michael a look and Peter arched a curious eyebrow.

"I'll make sure my team is copied on the call sheets as well," said Ellie.

"Wonderful." Peter exhaled as if a great burden had been released.

Ellie imagined him visually checking off a cluttered to-do list in his mind.

Peter clasped his hands in front of his chest and narrowed his eyes. "Now, on to the *serious* business at hand. How about an Al Cappuccino?"

Ellie raised her eyebrows, shocked. *What do you know, Michael's coffee names were already catching on.*

A huge grin filled Michael's face. *My first day in Hollywood and I'm already making an impression.*

"Victoria's assistant Ashley came up with that one." Peter chuckled. "That girl's going places."

Ellie's face flushed. *That little…!*

Chapter 8

The next two hours were a whirlwind of activity. The craft service tables were transformed into a battlefield of coffee cups, crumbs, random pieces of fruit, and crumpled napkins. Orders flew in from the production crew and the stars' assistants. The lead actors' assistants were always ushered to the front of the line ahead of the rest of the cast and crew.

"Chai latte, cold, skim milk."

"Gluten-free muffin—heated on *low* for ten seconds."

"Mango, strawberry, banana smoothie with chia seeds."

"Iced Caramel Macchiato, half-caf, extra shot, light ice, with whole milk, two pumps of vanilla, one pump hazelnut, upside down, extra caramel drizzle."

"Not too cold," another voice chimed in. "I'm not trying to go full Titanic here if you know what I mean."

Michael could have sworn Ellie grew an extra arm as she flew between the coffee machines and the blenders. Michael darted between coolers and the counter, arms full of fruit and oat milk cartons, wiping sweat from his forehead with his sleeve.

By the time the chaos ebbed, their inventory was depleted, and Michael's apron was sadly no longer perky. He leaned against the counter, catching his breath. "Fastest two hours of my life."

Ellie nodded as she wiped down the machines. The surge had finally passed—what little was left of their stock had been scattered to the masses. Her gaze shifted toward the floor-to-ceiling windows, outside, where ice still fell in sheets. Michael followed her stare.

"It's really bad out there," she said, a look of worry on her face. "I had no idea it was going to—"

"It's nothing." Michael reassured her. "I grew up in Boston. I'm used to driving in this type of weather—and besides, we're completely out of inventory."

Ellie gave a worried nod of agreement.

"You just don't want me to wreck your van," he gave her a mischievous grin. "You did get insurance on it."

"Michael," she fussed, "I'm already worried enough."

"I'm just teasing. I'll be careful, I promise." He pulled on his gloves, coat, and stocking cap. "Be back in a jiffy."

Ellie gave him a sharp look.

"Stop worrying, you've got a lot to take care of here," said Michael. "Call me if you need anything."

"I will… Oh—one second." Ellie reached up and fixed his collar. "Much better."

"Thanks." He grinned. "My mom usually spits on a tissue and wipes my face too."

"You're such a nut." Ellie laughed. She grabbed him by the shoulders, wheeled him around, and steered him toward the door.

"Subtle," said Michael as he walked away.

Ellie smiled to herself as she watched him pretend to fight the wind, staggering backward, arms flailing. It was all fun and games until he nearly clocked Gerald in the head.

She watched as Gerald wagged an angry finger in Michael's face. She couldn't help but smile. For all his silliness, Michael was a good man—and a good friend.

A sudden, unexpected surge of guilt coursed through her. She knew Michael had feelings for her—maybe more than she was ready to face. But the timing was wrong. Love was a distraction she couldn't afford.

Still, she wondered… *What if he meets someone else?*

Chapter 9

Michael eased the van into the Bitter Sweet Café parking lot, shifted into reverse, and backed into an empty space by the side door. He sang along with "Winter Wonderland" and cut the engine as the song ended.

Freezing rain stung his face as he opened the door. He stepped gingerly to the ground, bracing himself against the van, his feet slipping and sliding beneath him in every direction.

"I should have brought my ice skates," he muttered.

A smiling face appeared at the door as he approached—Olivia.

Michael waved and then kicked the ice and grime from his boots against the curb. He took a tentative step from the parking lot to the sidewalk, made his way to the door, and tugged it open. Warm air mixed with a blend of coffee and freshly baked pastries danced around him.

"Hello, stranger."

Olivia's usually neat blonde hair had escaped its ponytail, falling in playful tendrils along her neck and face. Her black shirt was dusted with flour. She hurried over and gave Michael a big hug.

"You smell like a cinnamon croissant." Michael grinned.

"I must look a wreck." Olivia sighed, patting her hair down. "I've been oven-hopping all morning."

"You look stunning," Michael assured her.

"I guess you're right." Olivia grinned. "Beauty is a burden I willfully endure," she said with gravitas.

"Somebody has to," Michael agreed.

"So, how are things going at the movie set? Met any starlets? Future Mrs. Wests?"

"The movie set is great; the mansion is breathtaking." Michael tilted his head as if reconsidering. "The statues are a bit garish."

"Ah." Olivia nodded. "And…"

"No sightings of a future Mrs. Wests," said Michael. "But if nothing, I am a man of great patience."

"I've always thought of you that way." Olivia laughed, motioning for him to follow her to the kitchen. "Ellie said you guys are pretty much wiped out."

"That's putting it mildly," Michael replied.

"Who would have thought the skinniest people in the world have the biggest appetites?" Olivia shook her head.

"It's all the caffeine. They just tremble the weight off," Michael explained.

"Tremble the weight off," Olivia smirked. "You're impossible."

"I've been called worse." He pulled off his stocking cap and scratched his head. His hair jutted out in all directions.

"So, we've got everything for lunch packed up and ready to go." Olivia pointed to a stack of coolers and boxes. "I guess we should reload the van, and then get you back to Ellie."

"Sounds good," Michael agreed. He was already beginning to have second thoughts about Ellie—alone—in such close proximity to all those stars.

"Oh," Olivia hesitated, slipping into her winter coat. "I'm sending Alexis over with you. Ellie said you could use the extra help."

"Alexis? You have a new employee?"

"Yes, Christmas hire. She started yesterday." Olivia zipped up her jacket and fished a red and green scarf from her pocket. "You'll have to give her some quick on-the-job training."

"Of course, of course." Michael smiled. "You *know*, my daughter's name is—" He froze. "Alexis?!"

Standing there was a beautiful young woman, with his same smile, the same mischievous sparkle in her eyes.

Michael dashed across the kitchen, wrapping her up in his arms, lifting her off her feet.

"Dad!" Alexis sputtered, her words muffled against his shoulder. "I can't breathe!"

He set her down gently, blinking back tears. "How—? How are you here?" His voice cracked. He hadn't seen his daughter in over a year.

When he moved to Lana Cove, Alexis had stayed in Boston with her mother and her friends. Soon after, she was off to college. Aside from a few scattered phone calls and emails, he'd hardly heard from her.

Michael held her shoulder, searching her eyes. "How did you even know where to find me? Is everything okay?"

"Everything is fine, Dad." Alexis beamed at him. "I went to your house, and you weren't there. Then I remembered you said this café was your second home. I Ubered over, and Olivia told me you'd be back any minute. The rest is history."

"You always were so smart. So good at figuring everything out." He looked at her proudly. "You get those traits from me, of course."

"Of course, Dad." She laughed.

"So, how long are you here?"

"The whole Christmas break."

"The whole break?" he whispered, his eyes filling again.

"Dad. Do *not* cry—you're embarrassing me."

"Sorry, I just wasn't expecting—"

"Michael West, if you start crying, I'll cry too," Olivia chided, "I'm a sympathetic crier."

"It's the fluorescent lighting," said Michael, dabbing his eyes with his sleeves. "I'm sensitive to overhead illumination."

Olivia muttered under her breath, shaking her head. She looped her scarf around her neck and tied a loose knot. "We better get moving before Ellie wrings my neck. You two can catch up on the way back to the mansion."

"Yes." Michael nodded quickly. "Of course."

Chapter 10

"I can't believe you came all the way to Lana Cove to see me." Michael smiled affectionately as Alexis slid into the seat beside him. "I've missed you so much."

"I've missed you too, Dad." Alexis returned his smile. She reached up and lowered the sun visor, checking her makeup. "You seem happy here."

"I am." Michael nodded, shifting the van into reverse. "I've made a lot of good friends... I really needed to get away."

Alexis nodded, caught up in her own thoughts.

Ice crunched beneath the van's tires as Michael pulled out of the parking lot onto Beach Street. Freezing rain pattered against the windshield, sliding down in rivulets, pooling like diamonds at the base of the glass. A transitioning palette stretched from the washed-out pale gray sky to the deep, churning gray of the ocean—cold waves breaking on the snow-streaked shorelines.

Gusts of wind whipped around houses and condos, rocking the tall van back and forth like a staggering drunk.

Alexis used the edge of her gloved hand to wipe the condensation from her window. "Reminds me of the Cape—you know, with the snow and the ocean. It's beautiful."

"It really is." Michael nodded, adjusting the heat setting. "So… you're here for your entire Christmas break?"

"Why?" Alexis grinned, punching his shoulder playfully. "You trying to get rid of me? Have some nefarious holiday plan?"

"No! No! Of course not!" Michael laughed. "You've always… well… I just thought you would spend Christmas in Boston…" His voice trailed off.

"Well…" Alexis brushed imaginary snow from the hem of her coat. "Mom has gone completely vegan."

"I see."

"And this year, Thanksgiving consisted of tofu turkey, mystery meat ham, and root vegetables. Dessert was an eggplant soufflé."

"Oh… sounds delicious." Michael grinned. "So, you're forewarning me of your expectations."

"A traditional Christmas dinner like you used to make, with all of the fixings."

Michael felt the warmth from his heart fill his body—he'd like nothing better.

Alexis lifted her phone to the window, snapping pictures of the ocean and the pastel-colored houses dotting the shorelines.

"So… where are we going?" Alexis asked. "Olivia had to take a picture of my driver's license. Said it's a big surprise."

"You could say that," said Michael, decelerating and coming to a stop in front of a towering wrought-iron gate.

Chapter 11

Michael eased the van to a stop at the back of the Marlow Mansion. Alexis was beside herself with excitement.

"Whose house is this? It's humongous."

"Evan Marlow," Michael replied. "Local philanthropist, mogul, media magnet, patron of the arts, etcetera, etcetera."

"And Olivia and Ellie are catering some kind of event or something?"

"We're on a movie set," said Michael.

"No way!" Alexis gasped. "Anyone famous?"

"Oh yeah." Michael laughed.

"Who?" Alexis unclasped her seatbelt, barely able to contain herself.

"One second." Michael glanced at the side-view mirror. "We've got to get you checked in with Gerald—security. A word of caution—he's a bit rough around the edges, but mostly harmless."

Michael slid out of the van and waved to Gerald, who huffed and puffed toward them, producing more smoke than a steam engine. He slipped, windmilled, caught himself, and kept going.

"Easy there," Michael called out.

Alexis joined him at the back of the van, just as Gerald came to a huffy stop.

"You're Alexis West?" Gerald asked.

"Yes, sir." She nodded.

"I need to see your driver's license."

"Sure." Alexis popped her phone case off and handed over her license.

After a cursory glance, he returned it. "Massachusetts, huh? Looks like you brought the bad weather with you."

Alexis responded with a placating smile.

"Here's your ID badge. Make sure you keep it visible at all times."

"Yes, sir." Alexis nodded. She flipped her phone and snapped a picture of the badge.

"You're going to want to put that away," Gerald said gruffly. "No taking pictures, and no posting to social media unless you are *expressly* given permission. Also, your phone needs to be on silent." Gerald eyed Michael, making sure the message landed.

Alexis blushed. "Oh—sorry. Yes, of course." She slipped her phone into her coat pocket.

"Make sure you explain all the rules to her." He gave Michael a wary stare. "All of them."

"Of course," Michael promised.

Another vehicle pulled into the parking lot, distracting Gerald for a moment. He muttered something under his breath and then turned back to Michael. "Explain the blue tape to her."

"Will do," Michael replied, nodding.

"Do not cross the tape!" Gerald called out as he marched away.

"What is his deal?" Alexis whispered as Michael guided her toward the doors.

"Not enough fiber." Michael shrugged.

"Alright," said Michael, grabbing the golden door handle and resting a hand on Alexis's back. "Prepare to be amazed."

Chapter 12

A whirlwind of sound and smells greeted them as they stepped through the doorway into the Dagmeyer Room.

Less than fifty feet away, the crew had transformed the space into a grand Christmas dining room. A cherrywood table the size of a car, decorated with red and white poinsettias, gleamed below a sparkling chandelier. A lush blood-red carpet woven with golden accents stretched the length of the set. Dozens of crew members scurried about, making last-minute adjustments for the shoot.

"Wow!" Alexis exclaimed. "They're building the set right there?"

"Yep." Michael smiled.

"Dad!" Alexis gushed. "This is epic!"

"Better than tofu turkey?" Michael laughed.

Alexis was about to answer when Ellie joined them. "You must be Alexis." She gave her a quick, unexpected hug.

"Oh," Alexis blurted, surprised. Bostonians didn't hug—certainly not on a first meeting.

"Sorry." Ellie laughed at her reaction. "There's a lot of hugging in North Carolina," she explained.

"Must be a new thing," said Michael. "I don't ever remember—"

"I'm Ellie," she cut in, waving Michael's comment aside. "I'm so glad to finally meet you. And… for selfish reasons, we really need the help."

"It's nice to meet you too." Alexis's eyes were already wandering around the room. "This place is amazing."

"It's a bit overwhelming at first," said Ellie. "Here, slip off your boots, and put these on." Ellie held out a pair of Sure-Grip shoes.

"Oh my!" Alexis exclaimed. "They're hideous."

"I know," Ellie agreed, "but you see that rug—" Ellie started, and then trailed off.

Both Ellie and Alexis turned just in time to catch Michael attaching a cardboard fig leaf cutout over the warrior statue's manhood, clearly in violation of the blue tape rule.

"Dad!" Alexis hissed. "The blue tape!"

"Sorry," said Michael, hurrying back to their designated zone. He eyed his work and gave a satisfactory nod.

"What is the matter with you?" Alexis asked. "You heard Gerald."

"Your father feels the statues are a bit emasculating," Ellie teased.

Michael draped an arm over Alexis's shoulder and gently turned her toward the far side of the room. "Ignore the statues," he said with a flourish. "The *true* beauty lies in the paintings." He pointed at a gilded frame containing a painting of a vase overflowing with flowers. "Behold, a rare Mozart."

Alexis puffed out her cheeks, releasing the air like a sad balloon. "Mozart was a composer, Dad. Monet was the painter." She gently slipped free of his arm and turned in a slow circle, taking in the enormity of the room. "So, the actors are going to be doing a scene there"—she pointed to the Christmas dining room setup—"and we're over there?"

"That's right," said Ellie. She glanced at her watch and gave Michael a tight smile. "We better get the van unloaded. Lunch is in an hour."

The trio worked in tandem with the film crew. Cables were taped to the floor, lights were hoisted and adjusted, and a woman with a tablet tested a mechanized camera, sending it gliding along a miniature track around the set.

The word on the set was that the dining room shot would be ready by four. Bitter Sweet Café was about to mix and mingle with the elites of Hollywood.

Chapter 13

"That's lunch," a voice called out. "Back in one hour."

Just like breakfast, the lunch crowd rushed in like a tsunami. Born and raised on Starbucks, Alexis was a quick study, helping Ellie with the drinks while Michael manned the toaster ovens, heating sandwiches and replenishing the stock.

There was a last-minute scampering about the table when the crew chief yelled, "Back in, everybody, back in—lunch is over!"

There was a last-second frenzy—the crew grabbing bags of chips and power bars as if they would never eat again. A PA's voice crackled over a straggler's walkie-talkie: "Talent on set, talent on set."

Suddenly, the atmosphere in the Dagmeyer Room shifted as Ian Stewart appeared, followed by Dillan Wiles, the film's second female lead. Fresh from hair and makeup, they looked every bit like Hollywood stars.

Alexis grabbed Michael's arm, trembling with excitement. "Dad, that's Ian Stewart, right there," she whispered. "He's *right* there."

"Yep." Michael chuckled. "That's usually what *right there* means."

"This is the coolest thing ever." Alexis wiped down a table distractedly. "I can't believe I'm in the middle of a movie set—"

"Yes, you are," said a distinguished voice.

"Peter." Ellie turned and smiled, recognizing his distinct voice. "Good afternoon."

"Good afternoon, Ellie." Peter nodded politely.

"You remember Michael, of course, my assistant." Ellie gestured. "And our newest addition, Alexis."

"She's my daughter," Michael added proudly.

Alexis sucked in air through her teeth, shooting daggers at Michael.

"Nice to meet you." Peter gave Alexis a practiced smile. "And welcome to our little piece of Hollywood."

"Thank you," Alexis gushed. "I love your tie. Is that a Salvatore Ferragamo?"

"Indeed, it is." Peter gave Alexis an admiring look. "You're a fan of Salvatore."

"I *love* Italian fashion," said Alexis. "Valentino, Missoni, Etro—"

"A woman with a refined palate." He smiled. "We may have to introduce you to wardrobe."

"A dream." Alexis smiled.

"Now," Peter smiled, rising up on his toes, "while I'm here, how about another one of those Al Cappuccinos?"

Chapter 14

Neil Phillips, a Ryan Reynolds doppelganger, strode onto the set.

Alexis gasped. Loudly. *My friends* so *aren't going to believe this.*

It was as if Adonis himself had descended from the heavens. He was joined by Ian Stewart, Noah Cruise, and David Brooke.

Even Ellie and Michael were starstruck—these were the biggest names in the business.

While Alexis only had eyes for Neil, Michael was drawn to the drama unfolding on the set. He had seen a lot of angry people in his life, and he could tell by David's body language, something was off.

"Somebody's in trouble," whispered Ellie.

Michael nodded, pretending to be busy organizing the snacks, all the while keeping a watchful eye on David and Peter.

"Now," barked David, throwing a stack of papers to the floor.

Peter said something unintelligible, grabbed a walkie-talkie from his pocket and stormed off the set.

Ellie joined Michael, watching the scene unfold. "That escalated quickly."

"Poor Peter," said Alexis, joining them. Ellie nodded in agreement.

"I wonder if it's—" Michael didn't get a chance to finish.

The double doors to the Dagmeyer Room slammed open, and Victoria Day swept in. She stormed past Michael, Ellie, and Alexis, leaving behind a trail of expensive perfume laced with cigarettes.

A skintight black dress played peekaboo beneath her ankle-length fur coat. Red stilettos flashed beneath her as she moved.

Peter Star followed close behind, his face crimson, jaw tight with anger.

David was seething. He shot Victoria a blistering look, but held his tongue. Instead, he pulled the actors into a quick huddle, his voice low and tight. Whatever he said was enough— the actors gave sharp nods and moved to their marks.

Moments later, a loud buzzer sounded.

"Quiet on the set," David barked.

Ellie, Michael, and Alexis froze.

"Rolling!"

Chapter 15

Michael watched transfixed as the cameramen and sound engineers moved in perfect harmony, like a technological ballet. A camera glided smoothly along a track, parallel to the dining room table.

Multiple boom microphones hovered just inches above the actors' heads. With so much activity going on around them, it amazed Michael that the actors could focus, much less remember their lines. Yet they brilliantly engaged one another: laughing, smiling, whispering conspiratorially as if the real world had faded away, replaced by their reality.

The flurry of banter between the actors lasted about four minutes before the director shouted, "Cut!"

Michael found the entire process mesmerizing.

"Did you see that?" Alexis whispered, turning to her dad. "Neil was amazing, and Victoria"—she grinned—"she's such a diva. I love her."

Michael nodded, still caught up in the scene. "Flawless," he agreed.

David lowered his headphones around his neck and gestured for the actors and cinematographer to join him. The cast gathered around the monitor to watch the playback. There was a brief discussion, a lot of head nodding, and then the actors returned to their marks, taking their places at the table again.

Only one person stayed behind: Victoria.

"This is ridiculous, and you know it," Victoria snapped, her voice echoing off the cavernous walls. "Ian should be sitting on the other side of the table. The lighting washes me out—and you said *I'd* have more lines in this scene."

David sucked in a deep breath as she continued with her tirade. The crew busied themselves, not daring to make eye contact with either of them.

"Remember when I talk about meeting Ian at the record store? We went over it—*again* and *again*—in my *trailer*."

Victoria's lips curved into a cool smile, making sure Noah, the cinematographer, didn't miss it. She placed her hand on David's chest. His face reddened as he brushed her hand away.

"We discussed this in rehearsal, Victoria," David said hotly. "The opening scene is you and Ian meeting at the Broadway production of

A Christmas Carol. I don't think our audience needs to be spoon-fed. You're in the opening scene for crying out loud."

"Well"—she shrugged dismissively—"at least move Ian to the other side of the table. It's preposterous we'd be sitting side by side. And get rid of that blasted mirror behind me—it's too distracting."

"Victoria." David's voice rose. "The scene stays as is. I'll flag it for a review. We're on a *very* tight schedule. Please *work* with me."

"And *how* do you expect me to do that when your expectations are unattainable!" Victoria shot him a scathing look, spun on her heel, and then stormed off the set.

David closed his eyes and drew in a long breath. He stood and motioned Peter over. An inky black silence spilled over the room.

"Tell Victoria if she's not back on set in *five*, she's in breach of contract. I don't have time for her prima donna antics today. This is her *last* warning."

The impact of Victoria's outburst was clear on everyone's faces. Ian threw up his hands and left the set to talk with his assistant. Neil Phillips spoke briefly with Noah and David, and then gestured toward the craft service table.

Alexis grabbed Michael's arm. "Be cool, Dad," she whispered. "He's walking this way."

Neil Phillips carried himself like a movie star: self-assured, cool demeanor. His perfectly tailored suit accentuated his athletic physique. His light brown hair with golden highlights was perfectly tousled—styled, but with a hint of mischief.

Michael met Neil's smile and stepped forward to help him when Alexis subtly pushed him aside. "I've got this," she warned.

"Good afternoon." Neil chuckled, finding Alexis's antics amusing.

"Good afternoon, Mr. Phillips. How may I help you?" Alexis smiled back, wishing her voice wasn't trembling. *Stay calm.*

Neil spun around and glanced behind him. "Oh, me? I thought my father was here." He arched his perfectly groomed eyebrows and laughed—a look, and a laugh Alexis had seen in dozens of movies. "Please call me Neil," he said, extending his hand. "And you are—"

"I'm Alexis, nice to meet you." She shook his hand, praying that hers wasn't cold and clammy.

"I've only got a moment before David lassos me and pulls me back on set." Neil stole a quick look over his shoulder. "I was hoping I could grab two Americanos?"

"Yes. Yes, right away." Alexis dashed off to help Ellie make the drinks.

"Would you like some fresh fruit? Homemade bagels?" Michael offered.

"No, thank you." Neil smiled. "They smell great, but just coffee for now. I don't want to have food in my teeth for the next scene." He smiled broadly, showing off his pearly whites.

"I didn't even think of that," said Michael. "Then again, I live the life of a hermit."

"I doubt that," Neil replied.

Michael stole a quick glance over his shoulder to be sure Alexis was busy. Against his better judgment, he decided to press Neil for a little dirt. "Miss Day seemed a little… upset. Is she going to be alright?"

Neil gave him a knowing look. "You noticed, huh?"

Michael shrugged innocently. "A bit of a casual observation. I've been known to dabble in the subtleties of human interaction."

Out of the corner of his eye, he could see his daughter mouthing the word *no* while dragging a finger across her throat.

"Have you now?" Neil glanced around to make sure no one was listening, and then leaned closer conspiratorially. "Let's just say, Victoria thrives on *chaos* a little more than the rest of us."

Michael arched his eyebrows. "I've known people like that. Makes things tough on everybody."

"We'll push through." Neil flashed a quick smile. "Actors are like puzzle pieces; you wiggle us around long enough, and eventually we fit together to create—"

"A work of art," Michael finished.

Neil chuckled. "I was going to say magic. But…" He tilted his head, a glint of amusement in his eyes. "*Work of art* ties in better with the puzzle metaphor."

Alexis hurried over, shooting her dad a look of equal parts utter dismay and betrayal. She couldn't believe he was chatting with Neil.

"Ah—coffee is here." Michael announced a touch too loudly. "I'll leave you in the capable hands of my daughter—uh, Alexis." Michael gestured awkwardly as he backed away. "Nice meeting you, Neil."

Alexis shot her dad a look that promised a swift and certain death before turning back with a radiant smile. "Here are your Americanos. I hope you enjoy them."

"Thank you, Alexis."

His eyes are so dreamy. She nearly melted as her hand brushed his. Did he feel it? The electricity that passed between them?

Neil glanced back toward the set. "I better get back. Enjoy your day." He lifted a cup in thanks to Michael and Ellie before striding away.

Chapter 16

Neil had been right. Slowly but surely, the actors found their rhythm. Puzzle pieces shifted into place, and the scene took shape. Even Victoria managed to make it through several scenes without a major outburst. She actually seemed to be enjoying herself, much to everyone's relief.

David made some minor concessions, moving the mirror and working with Noah to adjust the lighting, giving the set a softer, more golden hue.

As the hours dragged on, Ellie, Michael, and Alexis became pros at responding to the endless buzzers, bells, and shouted commands while quietly cleaning the equipment, preparing for the next morning.

"I've got a whole new respect for Pavlov," Michael muttered when the latest buzzer finally went silent.

"I know." Ellie laughed. "At this point, I don't even think—I just freeze."

"I'm going to be hearing bells in my sleep," said Alexis, covering a yawn with her hand.

Running on nothing but adrenaline, she was petering out. Her day had started at four in the morning, and now, nearly 7:30 at night, she was dead on her feet. At least the set finally seemed to be winding down.

Across the room, David leaned back from the monitor, rubbing the bridge of his nose. He beckoned Peter and Noah over. The three huddled together, trading quick glances at the set, nodding, murmuring, and then discussing more. Finally, there seemed to be a general consensus.

David stood, and rested a hand on Peter and Noah's shoulders. "Good work, everyone. We'll need to tweak a few things in the morning, but overall, I like what I'm seeing."

A visible wave of relief moved across the crew; it had been a long, exhausting day.

"That's a wrap for tonight," Peter called. "Get some rest—we'll pick up again at eight sharp."

Chapter 17

The winter storm had passed, leaving a trail of wreckage in its wake. High above, cirrus clouds stretched across the sky, streaks of gray and black painted across the canvas of a full moon. Wind whispered along the shoreline, spilling secrets into the night.

While Ellie and Alexis bundled into winter coats and boots, Michael started the van and cranked up the heat. The windows were frosted white, and the leather upholstery stiff with cold. Out in the distance, Michael could see the red taillights of Gerald's golf cart heading toward Victoria's trailer.

Michael tapped the dash display until he found a Christmas station. A smile tugged at the corner of his lips as he sang along with Michael Bublé, "There must have been some magic in that old silk hat they found." For a moment, he was a little boy again, nose pressed to his parents' picture window, watching the night sky, hoping to catch a glimpse of a sleigh pulled by nine magical reindeer.

Mid-song, Michael glanced out the passenger side window, just in time to see Ellie and Alexis stepping into the cold. He nudged the door open and quickly hopped out of the van.

"Watch your step," he warned. "The driveway has some icy patches."

He held the passenger door open for them, waited until they were settled, and then closed it gently. Using the van for balance, he skirted around the front and climbed back behind the wheel.

Three peas in a pod, snuggled together in the front seat—Alexis in the middle.

They hadn't even made it out of the driveway when Alexis's head tipped to the side, resting on Michael's shoulder. He tried not to move a muscle as he navigated the icy roads, not wanting to disturb her. Alexis hadn't slept like this since she was a little girl—and if this moment lasted forever, he'd be fine with that.

As they drove, Michael did his best to convince Ellie he should take her home. She was exhausted, and the roads were treacherous. But Ellie only shook her head, insisting that she had work to do at the café, and if things got too bad, she'd call an Uber. In the end, Michael gave in, realizing her mind was made up.

It was after nine when they pulled into Michael's driveway. Alexis slipped off to the guest room almost immediately while he warmed up leftover vegetable soup and brewed two cups of chamomile tea. He arranged the bowl, crackers, and a cup of tea onto a tray and then quietly carried it to her room.

Alexis was sound asleep when he peeked inside. Setting the tray aside, he gently slipped off her boots and pulled a blanket over her. Pausing in the doorway, he switched off the lights.

"Sleep tight, Lexie," he whispered as he closed her door.

Chapter 18

December 22nd 5:30 a.m.

It was still dark when Michael pulled the van behind the mansion. Alexis jabbed at the display, lowering the heat, her face bright red.

"I feel like one of those rotisserie hot dogs," she groaned.

"You were in control of the heat," Michael reminded her, pointing at himself. "Driver. And Ellie"—he gestured across the seat—"who's in charge of contemplating the subtle but complex nuances of life."

"Ugh," Ellie moaned. "How on earth do you have so much energy this early?"

"Simple." Michael smiled. "I embrace the majesty of each new day with open arms an—"

"He ate an entire box of Krispy Kreme donuts this morning," Alexis cut in. "At this point, he's ninety percent sugar."

"The *Hot Now* sign was on," Michael explained. "Impossible to resist—just like me."

"Gross," muttered Alexis.

"Traitor!" Ellie exclaimed. Still, she had to admit, nothing tasted better than warm Krispy Kreme donuts on a cold winter morning.

The trio piled out of the van. A fresh layer of salt crunched beneath their feet. Their breath rose in spectral tufts, curling into the dark air.

"No sign of the angry man." Alexis yawned.

"Hopefully someone's here," said Ellie, shooting a quick glance toward the mansion. "We've got to be set up by 6:30."

"I'll check the door," Michael offered.

With arms spread out like a tightrope walker, he made his way to the door and pulled. The door swung open with a *whoosh*. "We're good," he called out, giving a thumbs-up. He made his way back to the van and began unloading the supplies for the day.

Thanks to Ellie's feedback, Olivia had been proactive—pulling a favor by borrowing an industrial hand truck from one of their food distributors. The hand truck transformed into something resembling a giant wagon, cutting their trips down from dozens to three.

Inside the mansion, the Dagmeyer Room was cloaked in shadows, lit by a scattered array of dim overhead lights. Soft strains of classical Christmas music delicately danced through the air—sleigh bells and timpani hinting at festivities yet to come.

"Good morning." Peter's distinct singsong voice cut through the darkness, startling them as they set up their mini café. He paused by an elaborate panel of circular knobs, twisting them one by one until the room bloomed with light.

"Good morning, Peter," said Ellie, waving a hello.

"You've outdone yourself." Alexis smiled, admiring Peter's colorful tie. "Jerry Garcia?"

"The one and only." Peter nodded. "And look at this." He flipped his tie over, revealing a handwritten *J.G.*

"He signed it?" Alexis gasped. "That's so cool!"

"I know." Peter grinned like a little boy. "I was an AD on a documentary about his life. He gave me this tie at the wrap party."

"It makes quite the statement," said Alexis.

"Thank you, Alexis. Now—time to inspect the troops." Peter strolled the length of the tables, pausing to read Michael's apron. "I'm on Santa's naughty list," he read aloud. "Oh my." He chuckled.

"I was going to wear my mistletoe apron," Michael said, "but I felt some of the cast may find me too irresistible."

"Aha, that would be my concern as well," Peter smirked.

"I apologize." Ellie cut her eyes at Michael. "I'd fire him, but good help is hard to find."

"More than you can imagine," Peter replied with a dry smile. He paused a beat and then continued. "Alright—looks like you've got everything under control here."

"We'll be ready to go by six-thirty," Ellie confirmed.

"Perfect. Crew and talent will be rolling in any minute now." He glanced at his watch. "Let's hope for a less eventful day."

"I hope everything goes wonderfully." Ellie smiled, handing him an Al Cappuccino.

"And…" Michael slid in beside her. "Your gluten-free raisin bagel with a side of blueberries and strawberries."

"Color me impressed. Bitter Sweet Café—perfection, no notes." Peter gave them a thumbs-up, and headed toward the set.

Moments later, Neil Phillips, Ian Stewart, and Dillan Wiles ambled up to the craft service table as if out for a Sunday stroll. Neil sported a Red Sox baseball cap, Ian's hair was a tussled mess, and Dillan's golden mane was piled atop her head, cinched in place with a glittery scrunchy.

David, dressed in a colorful Christmas sweater and green slacks, followed close behind. His reading glasses clung to the tip of his nose, defying gravity as he spoke animatedly into his phone. He gave a quick nod to Peter, who was busy speaking with Noah and a heavyset woman wearing headphones.

As they reached the table, Ian—ever the perfect British gentleman, motioned for Dillan to order first.

Neil playfully peeked around her shoulder, "Morning, Alexis," he said with a wave.

Alexis felt her cheeks and ears flush red. "Good, morning Neil. Love the baseball cap."

"A little bird told me you were from Boston."

"Ahem," Dillan cleared her throat. "Trying to order here; some of us need hair and makeup." She gave Alexis a quick wink.

"My apologies." Neil grinned.

"Boys." Dillan sighed.

"I know; they're exasperating." Alexis laughed, cutting her eyes at Michael.

Dillan placed her order—a vanilla latte with oat milk—and then lingered at the table, filling a small plate with fruit and snagging a cup of peach yogurt and granola.

The espresso machine hissed to life, filling the air with the deep, nutty aroma of fresh grounds. A steady stream of rich espresso flowed into the cup. Ellie swirled oat milk in a steel pitcher until it turned silky, then poured it over the espresso, finishing with a drizzle of vanilla syrup.

"That looks delicious," Dillan moaned.

"Thank you," Ellie said with a smile. "Would you like a dusting of cinnamon?"

"Do angels have wings?" Dillan replied, her eyes lighting up.

While Dillan admired her latte, Michael set about making a creation of his own. He dropped an Earl Grey teabag into a mug of steaming water, added a splash of steamed milk, and finished with a touch of vanilla.

"Thank you, mate," said Ian. "This will do the trick—got a bit of a scratchy throat this morning."

"The air is a bit dry in here," said Michael. "I could add a few drops of honey. It'll do wonders for your throat."

"I appreciate that, thank you."

"Of course." Michael smiled as he poured honey into a small paper cup and set a tiny wooden stirrer inside. "This way you can add as much as you'd like."

"I'll catch up with you in a minute," said Neil, waving Ian on. Ian shot him a curious look before sauntering off.

Neil turned back to Alexis, locking eyes with her. She suddenly became very aware of her heart pounding in her chest. "How would you like a quick tour of the set during lunch today? Nothing major, just a little behind-the-scenes peek."

"That would be amazing," Alexis gushed—then her face fell. "But I can't really leave them on their own."

"Fifteen minutes tops," Neil promised with an easy grin.

Alexis held up a finger. "One sec." She hurried over to Ellie, whispering dramatically. A huge smile spread over Ellie's face as she nodded.

"Thank you!" Alexis gave Ellie an unexpected hug and rushed back to Neil.

"Yes." She nodded breathlessly.

"Wonderful." Neil laughed. "It's settled then—see you at lunch."

He gave Michael and Ellie a polite wave, then turned toward the set—only to double back when it occurred to him that Michael was holding his Americano and cold oats breakfast bowl.

"Almost forgot!" Neil groaned, rolling his eyes at himself. He scooped up the food with a grin. "Alright, this time, I'm really leaving."

"How'd I do?" Michael asked as Neil walked away. "I was quiet, no interruptions."

"There's hope for you yet," Alexis said, smiling at her dad.

Chapter 19

The morning was perfect—until it wasn't.

Michael had just passed four black coffees to impatient crew members when across the room he saw Peter's face fill with anger. The red rose from his collar to his cheeks like a cartoon thermometer.

Michael nudged Ellie's shoulder. "Look at Peter," he whispered.

Peter yanked his coat from a chair, shrugged it on, and with his phone pressed to his ear, he stormed across the Dagmeyer Room. All eyes were on him as he flung the doors open. Slipping and sliding on the icy pavement, he made his way to the security shack where he absconded with Gerald's golf cart. He spun the vehicle around and in a spray of ice and slush headed down the beach toward Victoria's trailer.

"Oh man," Michael whispered. "This doesn't look good."

"Where's Peter going?" Alexis asked, hurrying up beside them.

"Victoria's trailer," said Ellie.

Seconds later, Gerald burst from the security shack. His boots shot out from under him, leaving him clinging to the doorframe. He fought valiantly to right himself, but lost the battle, crashing down hard on his backside.

An audible "Ohh" rippled through the crew.

Not to be deterred, Gerald rolled over onto all fours, got his feet under him, and lurched into a run-limp after Peter.

A smattering of applause filled the room.

"Well," said Ellie dryly, "if nothing else, it's never dull."

"Did you see Peter's face though?" Alexis asked, eyes wide. "This is bad, right? I mean… after yesterday."

"I'd say so," said Ellie. "David made it clear he wasn't going to put up with any more of her theatrics."

"Do you think she'll get fired?"

"Hard to tell," said Michael. "That would set them way behind." He shook his head. "One thing for sure, we're in for another tense day on set."

A shrill bell rang out, startling the trio.

"Forty minutes, people," a crew chief barked. "Do what you need to do."

"Get ready," Ellie warned.

The room erupted into motion. A riot of crew members swarmed the craft service table, stuffing their pockets with snacks, and calling out last-minute drink orders. Assistants checked and double-checked their phones, receiving last-minute requests from the stars.

"Excuse me. Excuse me," barked a woman with jet-black hair and severe bangs.

"It's Chavon," someone whispered. The crew parted like the Red Sea as she swept to the front of the line. She locked eyes with Ellie, who froze mid-step.

"Caramel macchiato. Room temperature," she demanded, letting her eyes sweep the room, basking in the attention. "Victoria has *very* sensitive lips."

"Right." Ellie nodded, hurrying to the espresso machine.

"*Room* tem-per-a-ture," Chavon repeated, stretching the word into four distinct syllables.

"Understood," Ellie called back over her shoulder, biting her tongue.

Michael zigzagged behind Ellie, restocking the fresh fruit and pastries while Alexis helped serve drinks to the waiting cast and crew.

"Macchiato, *room* temperature." Ellie smiled tightly, delivering the beverage.

Chavon gave her a skeptical look, lifted the lid, and proceeded to pour a few drops onto her wrist. She blew, sniffed, and then finally declared, "It'll suffice."

"Wonderful." Ellie forced a smile and turned to help Michael.

"Don't you dare turn your back on me. Get me a napkin."

"Here you go," Michael quickly handed Chavon a napkin before Ellie vaulted the table and strangled her.

Chavon gave Michael a tight smile. "Glad to see someone's on their game." She huffed, spun on her heel, and marched off.

"Who in the world—" Michael started.

"Chavon," a crew member whispered, leaning in close. "Victoria's publicist. Cross her, and she'll make your life a living hell."

"I *believe* you," Michael said dryly.

A voice boomed over the room. "Thirty minutes to roll!"

If Peter's face reflected how the day was going, David's looked like he was having an out-of-body experience. He slid off the stool and bolted across the room, out into the cold, headphone cable snaking behind him. In the distance, sirens carved through the dark morning—Peter's wish would not come true.

Chapter 20

Crew members and actors crowded the high arching windows as a stream of blue-and-gray Lana Cove police SUVs barreled down the beach access road. Snow sprayed from beneath their tires as they fishtailed across the sand, blue lights strobing. Peter, David, and Gerald stood huddled together, watching as officers spilled out of their cars.

The entire scene was surreal. Behind the trailer, the sun rising above the water—looking like a freshly sliced orange—seemed at odds with the murky gray ocean, its golden streaks stretching out just short of the shoreline.

A stocky man emerged from his vehicle, surveying the scene as officers closed ranks around him. Immediately, he took charge, pointing and gesturing. Yellow tape was unfurled, securing the perimeter around the trailer.

"I think that's Louie," said Ellie, pressing her face to the window. She was referring to Olivia's uncle, Detective Louie Adams.

Gerald ducked under the tape; he hadn't taken two steps before the detective whirled on him. Gerald froze, backtracked, and awkwardly slipped back under the tape.

"Yep," Michael agreed. "Definitely Louie." He watched as the broad-shouldered man slipped on a pair of booties and latex gloves and headed toward the trailer.

Alexis slipped her phone from her pocket and zoomed in on the trailer. Her breath caught. "Dad," she whispered, touching his hand. She angled her phone so he could see the screen. Victoria was slumped upright against the door, her body frozen, her face eerily still.

"Dear God." Michael tightened his grip on Alexis's hand, his voice low and shaken. He slipped his other hand to Ellie's back, leaning in, he whispered softly into her ear, "It's Victoria… she's dead."

Shockwaves of emotion rippled through the crowd as everyone realized what was happening. Noah and several actors hurried across the Dagmeyer Room, pushing through the tall doors that connected it to the house proper, returning moments later bundled in coats and hats, hurrying to get outside and join the others at the crime scene.

Suddenly, there was a loud squelch. A sharp voice cut through the mayhem. "Everyone, everyone, please return to set—now!"

Kyle Makita—the Key PA Ellie had met briefly—stood by the dining room table, radio in one hand, a black plastic trash bag in the other.

"Move it, people."

Reluctantly, the crowd peeled away from the windows and drifted back toward the set, the excited hum of voices falling into an uneasy hush.

"Are we considered people?" Alexis whispered.

"I believe it's just cast and crew," said Ellie. "We'll just wait here—unless he calls us over."

"I've just spoken with David," Kyle announced. He shook the trash bag open. "Due to the current situation, I'm going to need *everyone's* phone."

A chorus of groans rippled across the room.

"I know," Kyle said in a firm but sympathetic tone. "These are David's orders. Anyone found with a phone will be off this production."

"Kyle, what about our families?" a voice called out. "It's Christmastime."

Kyle's expression softened, though only slightly. "I realize that, Tony, and believe me, I hate to do this." He lifted the bag higher. "But for now, I need your phones."

Chapter 21

Detective Adams paused in the vestibule. His cheeks red and ruddy from the cold. His eyes swept the cavernous room, taking in every detail—until they met Ellie's.

Ellie felt the weight of his stare and gave him an awkward wave. In return, he gave the subtlest of nods. His eyes shifted, landing on Michael. Detective Adams frowned as if he'd been offered a gluten-free donut.

"I think he's happy to see me," Michael whispered to Ellie from the side of his mouth.

He turned to the officers gathered around him, speaking to them in hushed tones. David, Peter, and the others were ushered over to the set, while Detective Adams made his way to the craft service table.

Ellie hurried over to meet him, handing him a cup of black coffee. "Morning, Louie."

"Morning, El," he grumbled. "Olivia told me you were working the Marlow shoot."

Ellie nodded. "Was going great, until…" She let her voice fade out.

Detective Adams nodded and sighed. "Horrible, and right at Christmas." He shot a piercing look at Michael. "Every time someone dies under suspicious conditions…"

"Nice to see you too, Louie," said Michael.

Detective Adams was about to say something that would be considered impolite in social gatherings when Ellie touched his sleeve. "And this is Michael's daughter, Alexis."

"Oh. Uh…" Detective Adams said, recalibrating, momentarily caught off guard. "Nice to meet you, Alexis." His voice tapered from a growl to a low grumble.

"Thank you." Alexis smiled. "You too, sir."

His eyes flickered to the set, where the cast and crew sat waiting expectantly. "I'm going to go sort things out. I'll be back in a bit. Thank you for the coffee."

He gave Ellie a smile, revealing yellowed teeth—stained from coffee and cigars— reminding her that she needed to make a trip to the dentist. He turned to walk away when Ellie softly called out to him.

"Louie, would it be okay if Michael runs back to the café to grab supplies?"

Detective Adams turned, his eyes traveling from Ellie to Michael, reading his apron. He breathed loudly through his nose, running his tongue over chapped lips.

"Olivia's already packed everything," Ellie added. "And these people are going to need food."

Detective Adams thought for a moment, and then leaned across the counter, the tip of his tie hovering dangerously over a silver serving dish of yogurt. "You go straight to the café. No detours, no talking to anyone," he warned.

"Straight there and back," said Michael.

Detective Adams's brow furrowed. "Don't go poking your nose into things. I mean it."

"I think we know each other well enough, sir—"

"That's what I'm afraid of." He held Michael's stare and then turned to Alexis, smiling. "Alexis, pleasure to meet you. Welcome to Lana Cove."

Chapter 22

Michael wasn't fooling anyone when he grabbed a cup of black coffee and bagged a bacon, egg and cheese croissant from the toaster oven. Ellie knew the bargaining power of hot food on a cold winter's day.

Michael climbed into the icy cold van and started the engine. A plume of smoke rose from the tailpipe. He glanced out the side window as a white van—the words Lana Cove CSU in blue on its side—slowly made its way down the beach access road toward Victoria's trailer.

Was she murdered? Overdose? She certainly had a lot of enemies.

Michael grabbed the coffee and the bag with the croissant and hopped out of the van. He walked the length of the vehicle, stopping at the back corner. From his position, he could see directly into the Dagmeyer Room. Detective Adams was addressing the crew, his back toward Michael.

Perfect. Michael quickly crossed the driveway and knocked on Gerald's door. Seconds later, the door swung open.

"Oh, it's you." Michael couldn't tell if he was relieved or upset.

"I come bearing gifts." He handed Gerald the coffee and croissant. "Thought you could use it after this morning."

Gerald nodded. He seemed to have lost a bit of his gusto. "Thanks," he muttered, reaching for the handle to shut the door. Michael blocked it with his foot.

"I was talking with Louie," said Michael, guiding the conversation.

"Louie?" Gerald gave him a confused look.

"Detective Adams." Michael chuckled softly. "Sorry—habit. We've worked a few cases together."

"You?" Gerald scoffed. "That'll be the day." He gave Michael a dubious once-over.

"Sure, check the local papers, I helped solve the murder at the Lana Cove Museum—"

"Look," Gerald cut in, his tone hardening. "I don't have time for whatever game you're playing. I've got enough on my mind."

"I'm serious." Michael reached into his pocket, pulled out his wallet, and flipped it open (a move he had practiced endlessly in front of his bedroom mirror) to reveal his private investigator credentials and badge.

Gerald examined the ID card, then gave him a short nod. "Impressive. Look, Mr. West—"

"Michael."

"There's nothing you can do here." Gerald's eyes settled on Victoria's trailer. "She froze to death, plain and simple."

Michael could hear it in Gerald's voice—something unsaid, something heavy. "You think there's more to it, don't you?"

"Maybe…"

"Come on," Michael pressed gently. "Your gut's telling you something, isn't it?"

Gerald shook his head, but his eyes betrayed him. "I think she went out with friends, got drunk, and passed out on the porch."

"She'd have to be really drunk… and don't you guys take her back to her trailer in the golf cart?" Michael frowned. "Certainly whoever was on duty would have made sure she got in her trailer okay."

"I don't know what happened. Usually, we keep track of everything in the log." Gerald's face tightened, his cheeks rigid. "She was just lying there… staring at nothing."

"I'm sorry you had to see that," Michael said softly. "I just get the sense that there's more. I know you might not believe me, but I really *am* here to help you."

Gerald nodded slowly. "I was on the force in Meyer's Cove for twenty years." Michael shook his head, unsure. "It's just a dot on the map," said Gerald. "Population seven thousand… we never had anything like this."

Michael's gaze drifted toward Victoria's trailer, the yellow police tape fluttering in the wind. "I still don't understand how no one noticed. I mean, don't you guys do rounds every hour?"

"Yes." Gerald hesitated, the look of someone wrestling with whether to speak. "Taylor came on at six-thirty last night. I went over the logbook with him—"

"Logbook?" Michael asked.

"We write a quick sentence or two about what we notice on our rounds: an unknown car parked across the street, someone loitering near the property. Everything gets entered and timestamped."

"And everything was normal?"

"No," Gerald admitted. "Taylor was asleep when I came in for my shift this morning… and then, well… all hell broke loose."

Michael was about to ask another question when his phone vibrated. He fished it from his pocket—there was a text from Ellie. *Louie wants to know if you're interfering with an active investigation.*

"Everything okay?" asked Gerald. "You look like you've seen a ghost."

"Yeah. Yeah," said Michael. "They need me back at the shop. Listen—how about we keep our conversation between us?"

Gerald nodded. "Probably for the best… for both of us."

"If you think of anything, shoot me a text. You've got my number." Michael smiled and patted Gerald's shoulder. "I'll bring you some fresh cinnamon buns and a homemade chicken pot pie—Ellie's mother's award-winning recipe."

"Thank you." Gerald gave Michael a whisper of a smile as he closed the door.

Chapter 23

Ink black shadows spilled across the shoreline. In the distance, a lone ship moved across the horizon. The light from its cabin bobbing like a magical sprite across the water. Just beyond the ebb and flow of the waves, the lone trailer trembled in the wind. The orange lights Ellie had grown accustomed to seeing were no more. The CSU van had long since left, leaving behind a yellow border warning curious onlookers to stay away.

While Ellie and Alexis busied themselves cleaning and restocking, Michael began transporting empty coolers and hot boxes to the van.

Across the room, David, Peter, Noah, and Kevin—the producer—huddled together on a set of sofas.

A man dressed in a black suit and red tie entered the Dagmeyer Room. Silver tray in hand, filled with crystal tumblers, each filled with a myriad of colors. He placed the tray on the table and served each person a drink, starting with David.

The acoustics of the room were such that, if Ellie and Alexis were quiet, they could hear the better part of the conversation.

"We're not going to shut down. We're too deep in to scrap this," said David.

Peter took a slow pull from his glass, resting it on his leg. "Without a lead, we don't have a film."

"Not necessarily," said Kevin. "If you remember, Camilla Scott was in final negotiations, but she couldn't make the timing work. She already has the script, and according to Serena Vale—her agent—she's available."

"She's bigger than Victoria," David agreed, "and more bankable too. If she says yes, we pivot. We'll reshoot the early scenes and keep rolling on the rest."

"That's going to be a nightmare for continuity," said Noah.

"Better a nightmare than a shutdown," David shot back.

"Then we're all on the same page?" asked Kevin.

"I'll talk with Serena and then loop in Camilla," said David. "Let's make this happen!"

Alexis leaned against the doorframe and tugged on her boots. The door connecting the Dagmeyer Room and the house proper swung open. A tall, elegant woman wearing a black dress and red leather boots paused just inside the doorway. Her eyes swept the room and then alighted on Alexis.

I hope she doesn't want coffee, Alexis worried.

"Alexis?"

She eyed the woman as she approached, her heels clicking, blonde hair—the tips crimson—brushing across her shoulders with each confident step.

"Yes." Alexis smiled at the mysterious woman.

"I'm Kate—Neil's assistant. He asked me to give you this." She handed Alexis an envelope, her name scrawled in cursive on the outside.

"Thank you," said Alexis. "I love your nails," she gushed.

Kate's eyes dropped to her nails, bright red lacquer with swirls of white, dusted with gold. "Very Christmassy, right?" She smiled.

"Very." Alexis nodded.

Kate's phone buzzed; she glanced at the screen, and then gave Alexis a goodbye smile—hurrying off to do whatever Hollywood assistants do.

Alexis watched Kate for a moment and then tore into the envelope, removing a slip of paper. *Rain check? Here's my cell. Neil.* She read the note again. A smile, filled with wonder and delight, spread across her face. *Is this for real? Did Neil just give me his phone number?*

She slipped the note into her purse, shrugged on her coat, and hurried outside, running to the van. This was like a dream come true.

Chapter 24

Noah sat at the end of his bed and reread Victoria's text from the night before. *Chavon claims Camilla is here in Lana Cove.* Attached was a grainy photo of a woman in sunglasses and a headscarf, her face half-hidden.

Was this Kevin's plan all along?

Noah tapped the gallery app. He had been with Victoria the night of her murder, drinking in a local watering hole. She had been disguised, of course: a blonde wig, some big frumpy hat. Sadness filled him as he lingered on a selfie—Victoria kissing him on his cheek, mugging for the camera.

Was she volatile? Yes. Unpredictable? Annoyingly so. But when you were the object of her attention… she was mesmerizing.

Noah had lied and told the police the last time he saw Victoria was on set that evening. "Goodbye, Victoria," he whispered, deleting the pictures from the night before.

Chapter 25

Exhausted, Michael, Alexis, and Ellie trudged into the Ocean Deck Restaurant—a seventy-year-old landmark perched atop a weathered pier, extending some two hundred feet over the shoreline into the frigid waters of the Atlantic.

It was one of the truest examples of "don't judge a book by its cover." The interior looked uncared for—a haphazard collection of mismatched chairs surrounded scarred wooden tables, each topped with a roll of paper towels and ketchup bottles that looked like they had been there since ketchup was first created. The air was thick with the smell of Clorox and fried foods.

An elderly man and woman occupied a small wooden stage topped with a green shag carpet and safety railings. An odd assortment of Christmas ornaments clung to the side; a few unfortunate ones had fallen onto the floor—or tried to escape.

The woman clutched her walker with one hand—the legs of the walker decorated with strands of twinkle lights. She held a microphone in the other. Beside her, her partner—a beer in one hand and a microphone in the other—gyrated his hips, flashing a toothless smile at the newcomers while belting out "A Holly Jolly Christmas."

"Dear God," whispered Alexis as she stood frozen in the doorway behind Michael and Ellie. "It's like a fever dream." Every fiber of her being told her to run.

"There's Livs," said Michael, oblivious to Alexis's outburst.

Olivia waved to them from a corner table nestled beneath a giant swordfish wearing sunglasses and a sagging fishnet strung with seashells and starfish.

Alexis took a few tentative steps, the soles of her boots immediately sticking to the floor—making a sound like ripping tape with each step. "Dad! Why is the floor so sticky?" She froze again, horrified.

"It's all part of the experience—decades of debauchery and frivolity. You're literally walking on history."

"Doesn't feel like history," Alexis moaned. "I'm afraid if I take another step I'll lose a boot."

Ellie put a tired arm around Alexis. "You'll be fine," she promised. "I've been eating here since I was a toddler."

"And that's like fifty years," said Michael.

"Watch it, buddy." Ellie glared at him.

Olivia stood and waved them over. "I was beginning to think you got lost," she exclaimed. Michael leaned over, giving her a quick hug and kiss on the cheek. "Great." Olivia smirked. "Now I've got lipstick on my cheek."

"Sorry, we're running a bit late," Ellie apologized, giving her best friend a tired smile, shrugging off her coat. "Lots to tell you."

Alexis eyed her chair suspiciously, clearly having second thoughts about draping her new winter coat over it.

"The dance floor is empty," announced the old man, his eyes settled on Alexis. Much to his disappointment, she sat immediately, sliding her chair under the table. Not to be deterred, the octogenarian wearing a cardigan and stretchy forest green dress slacks left the stage to work the nonexistent crowd.

He sauntered over to their table, channeling Elvis, jutting his hips to the side. "I'll have a blue Christmas without you—"

"*Wee oh wee oh*," Mildred chimed in, singing backup from the stage.

"Thank you, Larry." Olivia laughed. "You look fabulous. Now get back up there, Mildred looks lonely." Larry winked and scooted off, swaying to the music, his Stride Rite shoes squeaking with each step.

"You know him?" Alexis asked.

"They were high school sweethearts," Michael joked—immediately regretting it when Olivia gave him a swift kick to the shin.

"They're the owners," Olivia explained.

"And they take requests," said Michael.

"Thanks," Alexis murmured. "I'll ask if I can think of anything from the 1800s."

"Well, well. Look who the cat dragged in," said a singsong southern voice.

"Mary." Ellie smiled. She leaned over Alexis, giving her a hug.

Alexis turned in her seat, taking in the visual spectacle that was *Mary*. Equally tall as she was wide, she had voluminous white hair that glowed purple beneath the naked ceiling bulbs, held in place by a row of bobby pins. She wore a pale yellow dress the color of old newspapers, a cardboard-brown apron, and a thin gold necklace adorned with a huge hunk of crystal.

"And who have we here?" Mary fixed her gaze on Alexis.

"I'm Alexis… visiting my dad for Christmas." She offered Mary her hand.

"And he brought you here?" Mary took her hand in hers and patted it. She looked at Michael and tsked.

Alexis felt her face redden; she wasn't sure how to respond.

"Look at you, turning red as a lobster." Mary gave her hand one last pat. "I'm just teasing you." She gestured to the room. "It's certainly not much to look at, but the food is delicious, the drinks are delightful, and the entertainment… well… the food's good." She laughed.

Alexis laughed. She was quickly warming to Mary and the quirky restaurant.

Mary turned to the table behind her and, with the expertise that comes with years of hosting, she grabbed a silver tray filled with glittery drinks.

"I took the liberty of ordering some drinks while I waited," said Olivia.

"Thank you, Livs." Ellie turned to Mary. "You've outdone yourself." She eyed her drink, served in a chilled martini glass, filled with a deep rich red liquor, the rim dusted white.

Mary gave a pleased smile. "My own creation. I like to experiment when we're not busy. Cranberry Sparkle Martini, garnished with sugared cranberries, crushed candy cane on the rim, and a sprig of rosemary."

"It's beautiful!" Ellie exclaimed.

"Oh, it's nothing," she tsked, blushing under the praise. She served Olivia and Michael, and then turned her attention to Alexis. "And for you, darling, a sparkling cranberry spritz with a dollop of whipped cream and crushed candy cane."

"Thank you so much. It's so pretty I don't want to drink it," said Alexis, admiring her drink.

Mary gave Michael a quick wink. He pressed his hands together, smiling with genuine warmth, and mouthed *thank you* to her.

"I'll be right back with the sampler platter," said Mary as she hurried off.

Alexis began to relax—maybe the Ocean Deck wasn't so bad. She snapped a picture of her drink—posting it to Instagram—and then double-checked her text. So far, nothing from Neil.

The Larry and Mildred show switched gears, moving the night along. Mildred tossed a pink feather boa over her shoulder while Larry tilted a fedora rakishly over one eye and launched into "Da Ya Think I'm Sexy" by Rod Stewart. Mary clicked a remote—a glittering disco ball spun to life, scattering tiny stars of light across the room.

Alexis watched, fascinated, and a little concerned that Larry was going to break a hip.

Across the restaurant, a bell jingled as the door opened. A gust of wind blew in, setting the paper towels aflutter. A large figure loomed in the doorway, his face uneasy and tired.

Michael looked up and smiled, waving the man over. "I invited Gerald."

Chapter 26

Gerald crossed the room as Larry gyrated his hips, shooting finger guns at him as he passed by. He gave the couple a polite wave before continuing toward the table.

Outside of his domain, Gerald's usual gruffness was replaced with an awkward warmth. He thanked Olivia and Ellie profusely for allowing him to join them, greeted Alexis with a stiff little nod, and shook Michael's hand.

Gerald dug into his coat pocket, handed each of the women a candy cane, and—after a bit of searching—gave Michael a melted chocolate Santa wrapped in foil.

"Gerald is head of security at the Marlow Estate," Michael explained to Olivia as Gerald shrugged out of his coat and sat heavily.

"Oh, impressive," said Olivia, giving Gerald a welcoming smile.

"I'm not really in charge," Gerald began. "I simply—"

"Nonsense," Michael cut in. "That place would fall apart without Gerald. The man's got the eyes of an eagle—wait, is it eagle or hawk?"

"They're both correct," said Alexis, checking her phone.

"I'm going with eagle," said Michael. "Much more regal."

"Michael's embellishing things a bit," Gerald said, feeling his face flush.

"Not at all," said Michael. "Gerald was on the Meyer's Cove police force for over twenty years."

"Oh, really?" Olivia nodded. "My uncle's been involved in several cases there—"

"Detective Adams is Olivia's uncle," Michael chimed in.

"That's wonderful." Gerald nodded. "He's sharp. It's clear that his men have a lot of respect for him."

"That's very kind of you to say," said Olivia.

"The three of us have helped him solve a couple of cases," Michael said, gesturing to Olivia and Ellie.

"Yeah, you said…" Gerald said, looking at the others, brow furrowing with disbelief. "He is kidding, right?"

"Wait—what?" Alexis suddenly tuned in, looking up from her phone. "You never told me—"

"It's nothing," Michael said quickly, throwing up his hands. "I got bored sitting around, writing my crime novels—"

"*Novel*," Ellie clarified.

"*Unpublished*," Olivia added.

"The point is," Michael continued. "I was bored and needed a little excitement in my life. Plus, thanks to our combined talents, we actually solved a couple murders."

"It's true." Ellie nodded.

"He's even been shot," Olivia added.

"*Shot*?!" Alexis sat back in her chair.

"One second, hon," Mary called from across the room.

"Dad." Alexis gave him a troubled look. "What in the world?"

"Sorry," Olivia mouthed, realizing she'd said too much.

"Don't worry." Michael smiled gently. "It was a *very* small bullet," he assured her. "And it's only happened once."

The table grew uncomfortably quiet. Alexis's eyes reddened; she took in a breath and exhaled slowly. "I'm sorry," she apologized. "This is all a bit overwhelming."

Olivia shook her head. "I should have never said—"

"It's okay," Alexis interrupted, catching her father's eyes. "You've changed."

For a moment, it was as if the world disappeared. Alexis's heart beat with a strange, quiet ache of loss.

"I had to change, Lexie," Michael said softly. "I didn't like who I'd become."

Alexis nodded slowly. "It's just… not what I expected." The words felt heavy, tumbling from her mouth.

"I get it." Michael smiled gently. "But, I think it's for the better, don't you?"

"Well… I like your new friends. I think they're good for you." She smiled back. "It's just different. I mean, I'm not used to seeing you so—"

"I was like those statues at the Marlow Estate," Michael said with a nod.

Alexis's forehead wrinkled, a questioning look in her eyes.

"Frozen," Michael explained.

"Oh, thank God," said Ellie, bringing a little levity to the moment.

"I like the new you." Alexis smiled, giving his hand a squeeze.

"Did someone ask for a shot?" Mary asked, breezing up to the table with a tray of sugar cookie shots. "Santa's little helpers." She smiled.

"Yes, please," said Olivia. "It's getting a little emotional in here."

Chapter 27

"So," asked Ellie, feeling pleasantly warm after the sugar cookie shot, "how did Michael convince you to join our little soirée?"

"I invited him," Michael chimed in. "Thought he might want to be around friends this evening, in light of what happened this morning."

"Alright." Olivia spread her hands wide, like a magician revealing a dove. "Someone *please* tell me what happened."

"Gerald!" Mary exclaimed, returning to the table with a stack of plates and a sizable serving dish. "I thought that was you."

"Hi, Mary." Gerald smiled, clearly uncomfortable with the attention.

Mary sat down the platter, filled with an assortment of seafood, sweet and tangy meatballs, stuffed chicken bites, and chilled vegetables.

She placed a hand on Gerald's shoulder. "A bit late for you, isn't it, darling? Karaoke ended an hour ago."

"Karaoke?" Michael raised an eyebrow, suddenly viewing his gruff new friend in a whole new light.

"Frank Sinatra reincarnated, this one." Mary laughed. "Let me grab you a drink and an extra plate." She gave his shoulder a friendly pat before bustling off.

"Gerald, you are a man of intrigue," said Michael, grinning.

Olivia smacked her palm on the table. "Before there are any more distractions— what's going on?"

"Livs, you know the actress Victoria Day," said Ellie.

"Of course," Olivia replied. "Everyone knows her—the Ice Queen."

"Well..." Ellie hesitated, glancing toward Michael. "She *died* this morning."

"Died?" Olivia's eyes widened. She was quiet for a moment, then asked the obvious question. "How?"

"We're not sure," said Ellie. "But from what we were told… she froze to death."

"Rumor is, she had too much to drink," Michael added. "Accidentally locked herself out of her trailer and passed out in the cold."

"That's absolutely horrible," said Olivia. "Are they shutting down the shoot?"

"I'm not sure," said Ellie. "We overheard David—the director," she clarified, "say that Camilla Scott will be taking over the role."

Mary returned, bringing the conversation to a lull. She slid a frothy brew, then a plate and silverware in front of Gerald. "Bon appétit." She smiled, giving the table a practiced once-over. "I'll be back in a bit to check on you."

"Thank you, Mary," said Ellie. "Everything looks amazing."

"You're welcome." Mary flashed another smile before hurrying off as a gust of wind bullied its way through the door, ushering in another group of customers.

"Great," groaned Michael, eyeing the group of senior citizens coming in from the cold. "It's the beachcombers."

"This time of night?" Olivia looked surprised.

Alexis glanced at the door, and then back at her dad, confused.

"They're a bunch of bullies," Michael grumbled. "They trampled my petunias and stole my *Welcome* mat—claimed I was encroaching on their territory."

One of the bespectacled old-timers caught sight of Michael. He pointed two fingers at his own eyes and then at Michael—the universal sign for *I'm watching you*. Beside him, Charlie Rosin stuck out his tongue, blew a raspberry, and promptly dislodged his dentures, sending them skittering across the floor.

"A man should be able to operate his metal detector on the beach without being threatened," Michael huffed.

"They seem harmless, Dad." Alexis laughed. "They're wearing orthopedic shoes."

"That's so they can sneak up on you undetected. They probably keyed my car," Michael muttered.

Ellie patted his hand. "It's alright. You want me to go say something to them?"

"No…" Michael said, lowering his voice. "It's fine."

"So, when do we find out if we still have a job?" asked Olivia, taking a sip of her drink.

"Well for now, the crew and actors are still at the mansion… so we'll continue to provide food for them," said Ellie.

Gerald placed his fork beside his plate, took a swig from his beer, and wiped his mouth with his napkin. "I don't believe Victoria's death was an accident."

Everyone froze, turning their attention to Gerald.

"And… I believe I'm somewhat to blame," he said softly.

"How could you be to blame?" said Ellie. "That's ridiculous, you weren't even on duty last night."

"No… but I broke protocol."

"Protocol?" Michael shook his head. "What, did you forget to charge the golf cart? Gerald, you're the most *by-the-book* guy I've ever known."

"I appreciate that, Michael. But I did something that I should never have done."

"Gerald, talk us through this," said Ellie, concern etched on her face.

Gerald nodded and took another drink from his beer. "When we first started shooting at the mansion, I received an email from Victoria."

"Victoria emailed you directly?" Ellie asked, surprised. "Not… Oh, what's that horrible woman's name, her assistant."

"Chavon," Michael replied. "She moonlights as the devil." He explained to Olivia.

"You're right." Gerald nodded. "Usually, requests come from the stars' assistants or from Peter. However, this request came straight from her."

"What did Victoria want?" prompted Olivia.

"She told me that I was *not* to keep a record of her comings and goings."

"You keep a record of those things?" asked Ellie.

"Everyone that comes and leaves the set. We keep a security log and write up an hourly report," Gerald explained.

"Seems harmless enough," said Olivia. "She probably just wanted a bit of freedom."

"You would think it would be okay, but David kept a tight leash on Victoria."

"And for good reason," guessed Michael.

"In the past, Victoria has had problems with drugs and alcohol."

"I think those problems are… were still going," said Michael.

"Taylor and I were supposed to keep an eye on her," said Gerald. "But she made it clear that if we didn't honor her wishes, she'd have me fired."

"She can't do that," Alexis burst out. "Sorry…" She felt her face redden. "You're good at your job."

Gerald smiled kindly at Alexis. "Victoria had a lot of power. Stars have been known to lie about security, crew members they don't like… you can be blacklisted forever."

"That's not right," Alexis fumed.

"I'm still not making the connection," said Olivia. "What does this have to do with Victoria's death?"

"I have seniority over the other officers at the mansion. I told them to turn a blind eye to Victoria's comings and goings. And I…" He hung his head in shame. "Falsified the rounds in the logbook."

A stillness settled over the table. It was Olivia who broke the spell. "Gerald," she said softly. "This is going to come out in the police report."

"I know." He nodded. He took a deep breath, his eyes searching his new friends' faces. "I don't want to lose my job. Can you help me?"

Chapter 28

Mary cleared away the dishes and served everyone a fresh cup of coffee. "Oh," she said, glancing back at her tray. "This is for you." She placed a Shirley Temple topped with a mountain of whipped cream and sprinkles in front of Michael. "From a secret admirer."

"Secret admirer? Oh." The beachcombers snickered and snorted, pounding their table like teenage boys.

"Can I at least have a straw?"

"Of course, darling." Mary smiled, handing him a straw from her apron.

"Uhm, Mary." Ellie touched her sleeve as she was about to turn away. "You may want to leave that kettle."

Mary arched an eyebrow, and set the kettle on the table. "I'll leave you to it." She smiled as she turned away.

Michael took a sizable sip of his Shirley Temple, closed his eyes, and rubbed his temples. "Brain freeze," he muttered. He turned his attention to Gerald. "This morning you said that when you arrived for work, Taylor—the other security guard—was asleep."

Gerald nodded.

"Was this normal?" asked Michael. "Did it happen a lot?"

"Never," said Gerald. "I've known Taylor for years. I've never known him to fall asleep on the job."

Michael nodded, thinking. "Even if you weren't logging Victoria's whereabouts, you guys were responsible for driving her back and forth from her trailer to the mansion, right? I mean, I never saw her trudging through the snow."

"Especially in her Christian Louboutin's," said Alexis. "Trademark red sole," she explained, seeing the curious looks of everyone at the table. "No way she'd be trekking back and forth in those."

"Good point." Olivia nodded.

"Yes." Gerald nodded. "It was our job to transport Victoria to and from her trailer. But that's the thing, Taylor doesn't remember doing that last night. The last thing he remembers is opening the gates for Peter, because he forgot his remote."

"His remote?" asked Ellie.

"The bigwigs and actors are all given a remote or codes to get in. The front gate isn't manned twenty-four-seven," Gerald explained.

"What time was that?" asked Michael.

"Taylor thinks it was after midnight… he said the night was a blur," said Gerald. "I found him asleep at the desk when I arrived at six-thirty. That's also when I realized the logbook was missing, and then shortly after, they found Victoria."

"Someone must have taken the logbook when Taylor was asleep," said Ellie.

"Which also means, they had to have known about the logbook," added Michael.

Olivia looked up from her notes. "Taylor falls asleep, and he can't recall anything after midnight. The logbook goes missing and then Victoria's body is discovered."

"Doesn't look very good for Taylor, honestly," said Michael. "A major movie star dies on his watch."

"He was fired," Gerald revealed. "The police told him not to leave Lana Cove."

"We need to talk to Taylor," said Michael.

"I'm telling you, he didn't see anything," said Gerald.

Ellie shot a furtive look at Michael, telling him to *let it go for now*. "What about CCTV? There are cameras everywhere. Surely, they—"

Gerald was already shaking his head. "Yes, there are cameras everywhere, however, they weren't turned on."

"Why not?" asked Olivia.

"Famous people don't like cameras revealing their dalliances, if you know what I mean."

"Oh… makes sense." She nodded.

"So, as far as we know, no one knew Victoria's whereabouts or if she was alone," said Michael.

"No," said Gerald. "Right now, the police are working on a timeline of events."

"Remember when Louie popped into the Dagmeyer Room and spoke to us?" said Ellie. "He mentioned Victoria died under suspicious circumstances. Any idea what he meant?" She turned her attention to Gerald. "Did you notice anything suspicious?"

"I thought it was strange that Victoria wasn't wearing a coat."

"Is that unusual?" asked Olivia.

Gerald nodded. "Victoria was rail-thin. She was *always* cold, always wearing a coat."

"Maybe she stepped outside to smoke a cigarette," said Alexis. "I saw her smoking a couple times."

"Believe me, if she was outside, she was wearing a coat. And before you ask, her trailer had two smoke alarms after her previous incident of torching a million-dollar trailer."

"Yeah." Alexis nodded. "I remember—she was wearing that Chanel faux fur when I saw her smoking," she clarified.

"Okay." Olivia made a note on the back of the menu.

"Plus," added Gerald, "where's the cigarette? Where's the lighter?" He looked around the table. "Why was her key broken off in the lock?"

"Why would she lock the door if she was going to smoke?" asked Alexis.

"The doors on the trailer automatically lock," Gerald explained. "For security reasons," he added.

"Let's say she went out for the evening, came back, and Taylor dropped her off," Ellie suggested.

"He would have waited until she went inside, he would have never left her on the porch and driven off," said Gerald, watching as Michael attempted to stab the cherry that had settled at the bottom of his glass with his straw.

"Can you think of anyone who would want her dead?" asked Ellie.

"Who wouldn't?" Gerald replied.

Chapter 29

A light snow was falling as Michael and Alexis left the restaurant. Alexis reached into her pockets and pulled on her gloves, crossing the pier to stare over the railing at the roiling ocean—cold and dark as the sky above.

Michael stood quietly, letting her enjoy her moment, watching as the powdery flakes fell on her stocking cap and wool coat, glistening like white diamonds.

She turned to Michael and smiled. "Do you have a boat?"

"Uhm, no. Honestly, never thought about it," said Michael.

Alexis nodded, held a gloved hand to her mouth and yawned. "Alright." She sighed, stealing one last glance at the ocean, "I'm tired, let's go."

They walked in silence to the parking lot, both absorbed in their own thoughts. It was nearly eleven, and they had to pick up Ellie at the café at five-thirty. Michael knew the next day was going to be rough.

Michael grabbed the railing, descending the steps to the parking lot. He stopped two steps from the bottom. Alexis saw it too.

"Beachcombers?" She laughed.

Michael's apple red Miata was completely covered in whipped cream. Several discarded industrial-sized cans lay on the asphalt around his car. Alexis pulled off a glove and scooped up a bit of the creamy white confectionary, bringing it to her lips. She jabbed out her tongue, taking a taste. "Definitely whipped cream." She grinned.

Michael used his arm and hand and cleared the windows. "They are such a nuisance," he muttered.

"So, what are you going to do about it?" asked Alexis.

Michael thought for a moment and then a mischievous gleam flickered in his eyes. He surveyed the parking lot until he found what he was looking for. A silver Lexus with the plate MANKAND. He pulled out his key fob, popped the trunk, lifted his spare tire and grabbed the jack and lug wrench.

Alexis stared at him wide-eyed. "Dad, what are you doing?"

"I think our friends had a bit too much to drink." Michael grinned. "I'm going to make sure they get home safely."

"Dad!" Alexis gave him a worried look.

"Just keep an eye out for them, I'll be right back." Michael hurried over to Charlie Rosin's Lexus. He slid the jack beneath the car and began cranking. The car creaked and groaned and soon, the rear tire had cleared the pavement. Michael grabbed the lug wrench and removed the bolts from the tire. He shot Alexis a quick glance; she gave him a thumbs-up.

Huffing and puffing, Michael made his way around the car. He removed all the tires and stepped back, admiring his handiwork. He stacked them on top of each other, creating a tower, and then motioned Alexis over.

Alexis put her hands on her hips trying to decipher Charlie's license plate. "His license is MANKAND?" asked Alexis.

"Man candy," explained Michael.

"Dear Lord," Alexis groaned.

"Quick, help me make a huge ball."

Laughing, they dropped to their hands and knees, pushing and shoving until they had created a sizable heap of snow.

"What are we making?" asked Alexis.

"The head of a snowman." Michael grinned. "Grab some shells and rocks." Alexis nodded and scurried off.

"Dad! Dad!" she called out. "They're coming!"

Michael grunted as he picked up the massive ball of snow and placed it atop the tower of tires. Alexis hurried over, holding out her hands, filled with rocks and shells. "Perfect!"

Together they created a frowning snowman's face and then, giggling like children, dashed across the parking lot to Michael's car. He backed up, hitting the windshield washer and wipers to clear the glass.

"Here they come." Alexis bounced in her seat, smiling.

Arm in arm, the beachcombers staggered into the parking lot, singing at the top of their lungs—until Charlie spotted his wheelless Lexus. Michael gunned his engine and flashed his lights. The oldsters jumped aside as he flew across the parking lot, sliding to a stop beside them.

"You!!!" Charlie screamed, shaking his fist.

Bespectacled, ninety-year-old Erskin Springer hobbled forward and kicked Michael's tire with his comfort loafer.

"Hey, I had nothing to do with this." Michael laughed. "It was some guy, white beard, red suit, said something about a naughty list."

"You'll pay for this!" Charlie yelled. The other beachcombers joined in, yelling some not-very-Christmassy words and making some very naughty gestures.

"Well, this has been fun." Michael smiled broadly. "Merry Christmas."

Michael sped out of the parking lot onto Beach Street, chased by an angry mob of octogenarians.

Alexis lay her head on his shoulder as he drove home, the full moon lighting their way. "I like the new you, Dad," Alexis whispered. Moments later, she drifted off.

Me too, thought Michael. *Me too.*

Chapter 30

Michael fluffed up his pillows and pulled his covers up around his shoulders, shifting his feet until he found the perfect position. He'd just disappeared into that hazy space between sleep and wakefulness when his phone chimed, jolting him awake.

Groaning in annoyance, he rolled over and grabbed his phone from the nightstand and squinted at the screen. *Gerald.*

One other thing. Taylor's thermos was missing. Didn't want to forget.

Michael frowned, rubbing his eyes, and then replied. *Maybe the police thought someone spiked his drink and took it for testing?*

No, it wasn't on the desk when I came in for my shift.

Okay, Michael replied. *Let's talk in the morning. Could be important. Thanks for the update.*

You bet.

He set the phone back on the nightstand and drifted quickly into a deep sleep. He felt like his head had just touched his pillow when Alexis's gentle voice awakened him.

"Dad. Dad," she said, gently shaking his shoulder. "Your alarm's been going off for five minutes."

"Huh?" He blinked groggily, rubbing his head. "Okay, thank you, Lexie."

It was still dark when Michael eased to a stop at the end of his icy drive. Icicles hung from his mailbox, sparkling in the glow of his headlights. Out of habit, he glanced both ways before turning onto Maple Street and heading toward Bitter Sweet Café.

Alexis hugged her arms around herself for warmth and leaned her forehead against the cool window, watching Christmas lights shimmer and blink across gutters, archways, and frosted trees and bushes. Inflatable Santas, snowmen, and reindeer swayed back and forth in the cold morning air.

As they neared the heart of Lana Cove's modest downtown, the streetlights glowed—each one decorated with giant wreaths and candy canes. Garlands laced with golden lights twined up the poles, casting the sleepy town in a soft, amber glow.

Michael eased his Miata into the Bitter Sweet Café parking lot where Ellie, Olivia, and a tall, thin man wearing an elf hat were busily loading the van.

He pulled into a spot at the far end of the parking lot, alongside a mountain of snow left by a plow. "Maybe we should wait until they're finished," Michael suggested, stifling a yawn.

"One hundred percent agree." Alexis nodded. "I don't think they saw us."

Michael dropped his head to his shoulder and began to snore. Alexis playfully punched his shoulder. "Come on, sleepyhead." She yawned. "Let's go."

"Good morning." Olivia waved from the rear of the van. Her cheeks were bright and rosy; tendrils of blonde escaped from beneath her bright blue stocking cap.

"Morning." Alexis waved back. She chased after Michael, who hurried to the side door of the café to hold it open for Ellie as she backed out onto the sidewalk, maneuvering a hand truck stacked with boxes.

"I'll get that," said Michael, nodding to the hand truck.

"Gladly," said Ellie, stepping aside.

"Is there anything I can help with?" asked Alexis.

"No." Ellie shook her head. "This is it. I just need to grab my purse and laptop."

"Aww," Michael groaned playfully as he guided the cart down the accessibility ramp. "That's a shame."

"Don't worry." Ellie gave him a tired smile. "You didn't miss out on all the fun; we still have to unload it."

"Someday, remind me to share with you the meaning of fun."

Ellie rolled her eyes and motioned for Alexis to follow her inside.

"Michael West," fussed Olivia. "Less talking and more walking."

Michael kicked the wheel lock lever, and together, he and Olivia began sliding the boxes into the van. "By the way," said Michael, hopping into the van, securing the newly loaded cargo behind a safety band to keep things from shifting and falling, "Gerald texted me last night. He said that Taylor's thermos was missing."

"He probably took it home," said Olivia.

"That's what I thought," said Michael, sliding out the back of the van and closing the doors. "But Gerald said it wasn't on the desk when he arrived, and found Taylor sleeping."

"Could be something," said Olivia. "He may have forgotten to bring it that day. Did Gerald say he saw it when Taylor came in for his shift?"

"I don't know, but I plan to ask him," said Michael. "If someone took the logbook and the thermos, then we know something nefarious is going on."

"Alright." Ellie's voice came from the front of the van. "We're ready."

"I'll let you know what I find out," said Michael, giving her a hug.

"Don't get yourself into trouble," warned Olivia playfully.

"Me?" Michael asked innocently. "Never."

Chapter 31

Michael was surprised to find the Dagmeyer Room buzzing with activity. Both Peter and Noah were giving directions as crew members scurried about the dining room set, adjusting lights and props. The Trans-Siberian Orchestra's "Carol of the Bells"—one of Michael's favorite songs—filled the room with a renewed surge of energy.

"Did I miss an email?" Ellie worried aloud. She flipped open her laptop and quickly scanned her emails.

"I checked this morning," said Michael. "I didn't see anything new."

"Yeah," Ellie confirmed, "there's nothing here." She glanced up at Peter, but he was deep in conversation with Noah. "Alright, we'll just set up as normal then."

Alexis's phone vibrated. Carefully, she slipped it out of her pocket. Her heart skipped a beat; it was from Neil.

Are you here today?

Yes, Alexis responded.

Great. Want to cash in that rain check at lunch?

Alexis giggled, doing a little dance, composing herself when she noticed Ellie watching her. *Definitely.*

A thumbs-up emoji and smiley face appeared. Alexis, unable to control her smile, responded with the same.

"Somebody is happy," said Ellie.

"Neil wants to give me that tour at lunch." Alexis looked expectantly at Ellie. "Is that okay? We missed out last time."

"Of course," Ellie laughed.

"Aren't you supposed to include me in this conversation?" asked Michael.

"Sorry, Dad. You're my go-to if I need money or… well." Alexis thought out loud. "That's about it."

"Another tender moment," said Michael, emphasizing the first letter of each word. "You see what I did there?"

Alexis shook her head. "Not really."

"He spelled out ATM." Ellie laughed. "Dads have it so hard." She gave Michael a sad smile. "Now get to work."

The smell of freshly baked bread, coffee, and the sweet cinnamony scent of apple cider filled the air. Ellie noticed the crew eyeing them as the delicious smell wafted over the Dagmeyer

Room. As if on cue, Gerald arrived, looking haggard.

He motioned Michael to the end of the table. "I may have found something big," he whispered.

Michael closed his eyes, wishing it had been a toothbrush. "What is it?"

"You remember the thermos?"

"Of course," said Michael. "Taylor's thermos. Did you find it?"

"I found this." Gerald swept the room with his eyes, and then slowly unzipped his jacket.

"Aren't you going to buy me dinner first?" Michael whispered.

Gerald gave him an annoyed look. "Look," he said simply, revealing a white paper cup inside a plastic bag.

Michael nodded. "We do have cups, you know."

"It's Taylor's cup," Gerald whispered. "I found it in the golf cart this morning."

Michael stared at the white paper cup. "So, Taylor didn't drink from his thermos?"

"No," said Gerald excitedly. "He poured it into a cup. If we could get this tested…" He raised his eyebrows, imploring.

Michael's brain snapped into gear. "It might have traces of whatever was used on Taylor… and perhaps Victoria."

"That's exactly what I was thinking," Gerald agreed.

Michael closed his eyes and exhaled. He knew he should turn the cup over to the police, but they were painfully slow. Forensic results could take days. "Did you touch the cup?" he asked.

Gerald's face hardened. "Are you really asking me that?"

"Sorry—I deserve that," said Michael, holding up his hands. "Give me the cup. I'll put it in our fridge. I've got a friend who works at Bramston Young University. They've got state-of-the-art equipment."

Gerald hesitated, then slipped the cup into Michael's hand. Michael had just tucked it into the fridge when Peter appeared, eyeing them both suspiciously.

"Morning, Gerald." Peter's gaze didn't leave Gerald. "Aren't you supposed to be making your rounds?"

"Sorry, sir." Gerald dropped his eyes like a scolded child.

"He was just getting coffee," Michael explained. "I'll leave it in your office."

"Thank you," Gerald said and hurried off.

Peter followed Gerald with his eyes until he was outside. He turned back to Michael, his lips curling into a smile that didn't reach his eyes.

"You two weren't discussing *Victoria*, were you?"

"No," Michael said, surprised by Peter's accusatory tone.

"Good." Peter's tone was crisp. "Just a polite reminder about the NDA you signed." He smiled mechanically again.

"No need," Michael said smoothly. "I know the importance of keeping things quiet—I spent years at an elite advertising firm in Boston."

"Mhm," Peter hummed, unconvinced.

"I know how important it is for you guys to get ahead of the narrative," Michael assured him. "You'll have zero problems from me."

"Peter!" Alexis called, racing up with a grin.

Peter's expression softened. He gave Michael one last measured look, and then turned, beaming at Alexis.

Chapter 32

An almost reverent hush fell over the Dagmeyer Room as Camilla Scott breezed in. Michael froze—the tapioca-covered ladle in his hand slipped from his fingers, clattering noisily against the floor.

Her hypnotic blue-green eyes flicked toward him, the faintest hint of a smile tugging at the corners of her lips. Soft waves of hair framed her face, a natural mix of blonde and dark golden tones that shimmered under the lights.

Unable to move, Michael's gaze followed her as she passed by—wearing a sleek black dress that hugged her figure, simple but stunning. A deep-toned green leather jacket gave her an edgy, but classic look. She moved with effortless grace—a woman who didn't need to try to be noticed; she just was.

Michael was jolted back to reality by a sharp smack to the back of his head.

"Put your eyes back in their sockets," Ellie hissed, clearly unimpressed by his sudden infatuation.

Alexis frowned, a mix of embarrassed disappointment flickering across her face.

"That's *Camilla Scott*," whispered Michael. "The actress!"

"Yes," Ellie shot back dryly. "And you have tapioca pudding all over your shoe."

"Sorry," Michael muttered, bending to retrieve the fallen ladle. "We just saw her new movie *Stolen Kiss*."

"I know," Ellie grumbled. "Unfortunately, *I* was there."

"Not a fan then?" Alexis asked, hiding a quiet laugh behind her hand.

"Don't listen to her," Michael said, "she was riveted."

"That's one word for it," Ellie replied.

"Anyway," Michael pressed on, undeterred, "Camilla plays a model whose lips are so beautiful that the company insures them for fifty million dollars. But a rival actress—played *brilliantly* by Scarlett Johansson—is jealous of all her high-end makeup endorsements, so she fills her lip-plumper with acid in an attempt to destroy Camilla's lips."

Alexis's eyes darted to Ellie, who gave an affirming nod, silently acknowledging that yes—the absurd plot was real.

"And *right* when she's about to touch the plumper to her lips—"

"My best friend slaps it out of my hand," came a mysterious voice, "saving my lips and burning a hole through the floor."

"Ah!" Michael yelped, his voice hitting a high pitch as he once again dropped his wooden ladle.

Camilla Scott stood between Noah and Peter—less than five feet away.

"Impressive vocal range." Camilla laughed teasingly.

Michael's mouth moved, but his words were lost—caught up somewhere in the ocean-blue swirl of her eyes.

Peter chuckled at Michael's antics, shaking his head.

"Camilla Scott," Michael blurted.

"I apologize," said Ellie, gently pushing Michael aside. "He was literally just talking about how much he loved *Stolen Kiss*, and then—here you are."

"Here I am." Camilla smiled playfully, her lips parting to reveal perfect gleaming teeth.

"What would you like?" asked Ellie, fighting to calm her own nerves—Camilla Scott was perhaps the most beautiful woman she had ever seen.

"If you could make this, you'll be my hero," said Camilla, handing Ellie her phone, bedazzled in a sparkly golden case.

"A Snowfall Latte," Ellie read aloud. She quickly grabbed a napkin, jotted down the ingredients, then returned Camilla's phone. "This actually looks delicious."

"It is—and it doesn't give me that sugar crash."

While Ellie hurried off to make Camilla's latte, Alexis tended to Peter and Noah.

"Would you like your usual, Peter?"

"Actually…" Peter hesitated; he'd been watching Ellie mix a myriad of intoxicatingly delicious ingredients: espresso, almond milk, vanilla extract, a pinch of cinnamon. "I'll have whatever Camilla is having."

"Okay." Alexis grinned. "I don't believe we've met." She offered her hand. "Alexis West."

"Noah Cruise. Cinematographer," he said, taking her hand. "Nice to meet you."

"Are those Persol 714?" Alexis asked, surprising him. "Keyhole bridge and acetate color—very Steve McQueen."

"Yes, they are." Noah chuckled. "Spot on."

"I've been testing her knowledge of ties," said Peter. "She's been three for three."

"She's got an eye," Noah agreed. "Maybe a future in wardrobe. Alisha's always looking for new talent."

Peter nodded. "I thought the same thing."

"Thank you." Alexis blushed, waving aside the compliment. "What would you like, Mr. Cruise?"

"Please, just Noah." He smiled. "I *was* going to go with a simple hazelnut and cinnamon…" He paused, glancing toward Ellie and Camilla. "But I'll throw my hat into the ring and have whatever they're having."

"Sounds perfect," Alexis chirped. She hurried off, joining Ellie while Peter and Noah huddled around Camilla, making small talk.

Michael's phone dinged, bringing him out of his starstruck stupor. He turned his back to everyone, and slipped it out of his pocket—it was a text from Gerald. *Anything?*

Working on it, Michael replied.

Keep me in the loop.

Will do.

"Be right back," Michael told Ellie quietly. "Restroom."

The Dagmeyer restroom was larger than Michael's master bedroom. A gold framed mirror extended the length of the room and beneath it ran a counter with three basins. Beside each basin, a handwoven basket was filled with toiletries: disposable nail clippers, emery board, razors, floss, and mouthwash.

Michael fished his phone from his pocket and fired off a quick text to his friend Abraham Leung at Bramston Young University, explaining the urgency of his situation and apologizing for being so cryptic.

He placed his phone on the counter and—while waiting for Abraham's reply—began digging through the bowl of toiletries.

Curiosity got the better of him. He pulled out a plastic shower cap and pulled it on so it was snug. Turning sideways to the mirror, he raised and lowered his eyebrows, admiring his reflection. He tucked a few stray tendrils of hair beneath the elastic band and then continued foraging through the basket. "Mhm," he muttered softly, discovering a pouch of Q-tips. He gently slid one into each nostril, snapped a selfie, and sent it to Alexis.

He followed up his text with: *I am the eggman. I am the walrus. Goo goo g'joob.*

A young ponytailed man wearing a headset hurried into the restroom and, upon discovering Michael, stopped dead in his tracks. He gave an awkward smile and began slowly backing toward the door.

"Sorry," Michael blurted, yanking off the shower cap. "Just sending a silly selfie to my daughter. I assure you that I'm not crazy." He smiled weakly. "She loves the Beatles—Eggman, Walrus…"

"Okay…" The man nodded, still unsure, still hovering by the doorway.

"I work the crafty table," Michael said, gesturing vaguely. "They're probably looking for me, I'm gonna get back." He scooped up the shower cap and the Q-tips package and tossed them in the trash. He gave his hands a quick rinse before heading for the door.

The young man stopped him as he passed. "Your tusks," he muttered, eyeing Michael's nose.

"Oh—right." Michael laughed. "Thank you."

Michael had just returned to craft service table when he felt his phone buzz in his pocket. He knelt, hidden away from watchful eyes and quickly read the message.

Can you meet me at Cracker Barrel off exit twenty at eleven?

I'll be there, Michael replied.

He slipped his phone back into his pocket, and motioned Ellie over. "There's a cup in a plastic bag in the fridge. Don't throw it away—it's evidence."

Ellie glanced at the fridge and then back at Michael. "Why is there evidence in our fridge?"

"Preservation," Michael explained. "It keeps mold from growing."

"No, I mean *why* is there evidence in our fridge?"

"Gerald gave it to me for safekeeping. I'm taking it to Abraham, so he can analyze it."

A look of horror crept over Ellie's face. "Is this Victoria's cup? Please tell me Gerald didn't steal evidence from the crime scene."

"Of course not." Michael reassured her. "Gerald found the cup in his golf cart. It's Taylor's, we're—"

"Everything okay over here?" Alexis interrupted, her eyes darting back and forth between Michael and Ellie. "I'm sensing a little tension."

"No tension," Michael assured her. "We're discussing some evidence Gerald found."

"You found evidence?" Alexis's eyes lit up.

"Gerald found a cup," said Michael. "It's in the fridge, so don't throw it away."

"Oh." Alexis frowned. "A cup… how boring."

"I agree." Michael nodded. His eyes met Ellie's. "So, there's no need to make a big deal out of it."

"I think we should give it to Louie," said Ellie.

"And wait a week for the forensic report? Abraham can have a complete analysis in a matter of hours," said Michael. "Then I promise you, I'll tell Gerald to give the cup to Louie, unscathed."

Ellie mulled over Michael's reasoning. He was right—Lana Cove didn't have the resources to handle things quickly, especially a high-profile case like this.

"Alright, I don't like it," said Ellie. "But, I agree."

"It's the right decision," said Michael. "I have to meet him at eleven at Cracker Barrel."

"Vile." Ellie held up her crossed fingers and hissed at him.

"What's a Cracker Barrel?" asked Alexis.

"It's where gluten goes to die," said Ellie matter-of-factly.

Michael knelt behind the table once again and quickly sent Gerald a text. *Meeting Abraham at eleven. Will update when I get back.*

Moments later, Gerald replied with a thumbs-up and a cow, followed by a lengthy explanation describing that the cow was an accident.

Chapter 33

Michael was just removing a pan of cinnamon buns from the toaster oven when David Brooke strode into the Dagmeyer Room, each stride carrying a sense of purposeful energy. Kyle Makita followed a step behind, his short legs doing everything they could to keep up. He nearly collided with David when he abruptly changed direction and headed straight to the craft service table.

"Here," said David, leaning over the table and thrusting an empty coffee cup into Alexis's hands. He turned to Kyle, issuing orders without missing a beat. "Tell Peter to set up the final blocking rehearsal. If everything goes right, we'll roll."

"Yes, sir." Kyle gave a curt nod.

Alexis caught a fleeting flash of disappointment cross his face. She felt a tinge of sympathy for the assistant director as he scuttled off toward the set.

David slipped his phone from his pocket, glancing at a text.

While the man was momentarily distracted, Alexis gave him a quick once-over: late forties, blessed with thick hair, and only the crisscross of faint wrinkles at the corners of his eyes betrayed his age. His Botox injections had done their job—his forehead was as smooth as Sade's vocals. A gold braided David Yurman bracelet flashed into view as he slid his phone back into his pocket.

"Flat White—extra hot," said David. He hesitated and then added a barely audible "Thank you" as Alexis nodded and hurried away.

Ellie grabbed a clean cup and pulled a double shot of espresso while Alexis filled a metal pitcher with milk.

"Steam it to one-forty," said Ellie. "He wants it hot, he's going to get it hot."

"May I get you anything else?" Michael asked.

"No, thank you." David's eyes slid down to Michael's apron, which read *Check out my buns* in elegant gold embroidery.

"They're cinnamon." Michael grinned. "Lightly dusted."

"Gluten-free?" asked David.

"Of course," Michael replied.

"Alright." David nodded. "I'll take a bun."

Alexis double sleeved the piping-hot coffee cup, popped on a lid, and handed it to David. "Enjoy," she said, offering a warm smile.

David returned a quick smile, scooped up the cinnamon bun, and headed for the set.

"No wonder everyone is so afraid of him," Alexis said quietly to her dad.

"He's not so bad," Michael replied. "I've worked with a bunch of people like him in Boston. He's probably juggling a million things in his head—and small talk isn't one of them."

"I'll say," Alexis murmured.

Across the room, the actors gathered around the dining room table for a final blocking rehearsal—one last run-through of lines and movements before filming. Outside, a horse trailer pulled into the driveway parking beside Ellie's van.

"Alright, everyone," said David, eyeing the set. "Final block. Let's walk it slow, find your beats, and we'll roll right after." He slipped on his headphones and took a seat behind a large display.

Peter cupped his hands. "Quiet on set! Final blocking rehearsal for scene twenty-three! Lock it up!"

The low hum of conversation faded. David waited a beat and then called out, "Action!"

Ellie, Alexis, and Michael watched silently from across the room. Would Camilla be able to bring the same energy to the set as Victoria?

"Oh, darling!" Temperance—played by Camilla—exclaimed. "You've got a little something on your mouth."

"Oh?" Brett—played by Ian—reacted in mock horror as she angled over.

Temperance placed her hand aside his jaw, turning his head ever so slightly, she gave him a long deliberate kiss. Rex Archer—played by Neil—added a comedic beat by checking his watch as the prolonged kiss continued.

"*Lipstick.*" Temperance giggled, grabbing a cloth napkin and wiping Brett's lips.

The other actors joined in a chorus of uncomfortable laughter.

Temperance stole a devilish glance at Rex, and arched a perfect eyebrow. "Tell me, Rex darling," she purred, her voice smooth and deadly, the silk of her dress slipping seductively from her shoulders. "What's Christmas like for…" she tsked and turned to Brett in a pout. "I can't think of the word… lumpkins."

Brett looked at her and shrugged, still recovering from oxygen deprivation. "I'm not sure, sugarplum," he mused.

"Oh, yes." Temperance laughed unkindly, as if she'd just conjured the word, "*unfortunate.*"

Her lips twisted into a Grinch-like smile. "What's it like?"

Rex furrowed his brow, as if seriously contemplating Temperance's question. "It's pretty much the same as here," he replied. "I mean, of course, after we slaughter the cow, pickle a few pigs' feet, and pluck the turkey, we—"

"Oh." Temperance held her napkin to her mouth, her eyes wide. "That's beastly," she cried.

"It's the circle of life, ma'am." Rex poked fun with his faux Southern accent. "And the line for the outhouse can be a bit tedious, but as long as you've got a good newspaper, you'll be—"

"I think I've lost my appetite!" Temperance exclaimed breathily. "I feel pale, darling." She turned to Brett, patting her face. "Brett darling, am I pale?"

"Speaking of pails." Rex smiled mischievously. "That's what we use in the—"

Chelsie Frost—played by Dillan Wiles—patted Rex's hand and squeezed. "We get the point." She cast a wary glance across the table. "I fear if you continue," she warned, "Temperance may implode."

"Alright," Rex surrendered, a look of mock concern on his face. "We wouldn't want that."

"No," Chelsie agreed. "I'd hate to ruin this Hermès silk—it's vintage, and my cleaner nearly cried pressing it."

Across the table, Brett dipped a cloth napkin into a cup of water and dabbed Temperance's forehead.

"I can't feel a thing," whispered Temperance. "Am I in shock?"

"No, darling. It's just the Botox," Brett assured her, softly smoothing back her hair. "Just the Botox."

Rex turned to the camera and gave a mischievous, playful smile.

"Cut!" David's voice rang out from behind the monitor.

For a moment, silence filled the room—then David broke into a wide grin. "That was fantastic."

"You have *me* to thank for David's change in demeanor," Michael boasted.

Ellie gave Michael a wary look. "Dare I even ask?"

"No," begged Alexis. "You dare not."

"Fine." Michael grinned. "If you insist—it was my buns."

"Dear Lord," Ellie whispered.

"I warned you." Alexis frowned.

"They're magical."

The crew burst into applause. Michael gave a discreet bow. Camilla laughed, brushing her hair from her face while the other actors congratulated one another. Around the set, the tension melted into cheerful chatter.

"That's the energy I want," David called out, clapping his hands. "That's the scene, people!"

Chapter 34

Michael wheeled into the frozen Bitter Sweet parking lot—the van's rear fishtailing as he plowed through a riot of ice chunks the size of softballs. He backed into the loading zone and cut the engine.

"Training for NASCAR?" Olivia asked as she joined Michael at the back of the van.

"Practicing evasive maneuvers from the beachcombers." Michael glanced over his shoulder as if they might descend upon him at any moment. "Word on the street is I'm on their hit list."

"Oh." Olivia gave him a sad smile. "Then I'm afraid your days are numbered." She moved aside while Michael wrestled the hand truck out of the van. "But really…" She let the words hang in the air.

"Bit of a time crunch. I have to meet Abraham at eleven at Cracker Barrel."

Olivia gave him a look that clearly said *Oh, how the mighty have fallen.*

"Gerald found some evidence—"

"And you're giving it to Abraham?"

Michael braced for the lecture, but Olivia's face remained surprisingly passive. "And…" he continued, "I knew if we gave it to the police, results could take days—maybe weeks."

Olivia nodded slowly. "And let me guess—Ellie jumped down your throat when you told her."

Michael nodded and held a finger to his lips. "Shh," he whispered. "She may still be there." He slid the last Cambro onto the hand truck and closed the doors.

"What did Gerald find?"

"A cup."

"A cup?" Olivia blinked, looking deflated.

"Why is everyone so disappointed when I say that?"

"Well… it's not very dramatic, is it?" Olivia shrugged. "Like CCTV of the murder, or a gun, or a bloody knife—*that's* evidence."

"She froze to death," Michael protested. "She wasn't bludgeoned, shot, or stabbed."

"Try harder next time." Olivia hurried up the ramp, holding the café door open for him.

"This cup," said Michael defensively, "may still have traces of whatever substance was used to knock out Taylor—maybe even Victoria. If Abraham can identify the compound, we can tell the medical examiner exactly what to look for. It could break the case wide open."

"And won't the ME wonder where you got this information?"

"They'll never know who called it in. It will be an anonymous tip," said Michael.

"Makes sense," said Olivia. "I'll run it by Uncle Louie."

"Oh, you're funny," Michael replied. "The beachcombers and your uncle after me—who needs enemies when they've got friends like you?"

Olivia laughed and gave him a quick hug. "Let's get you on the road."

Michael climbed the wooden steps onto the trademark Cracker Barrel Porch, complete with swinging benches and old tractor wheels. He held the door open for an adorable elderly couple who had seemingly merged into one—both dressed in matching red jackets, red gloves, and evergreen slacks. The word *Slugger* was embroidered in silver across the back of each jacket with a stitched baseball bat just below it—each of their names, *Charles* and *Lucy*, sewn neatly inside the bat.

As he waited for them to cross the threshold into the restaurant, Michael imagined Charles shuffling   toward   first   base—another octogenarian, ball in glove, chasing him down. Would Charles slide into first? Would Charles even make it to first?

Lucy turned mid-entrance and patted Michael's hand. "Thank you, deary." She smiled, revealing a beautiful set of dentures streaked with red lipstick.

Charles glared at Michael, giving him the stink eye, before grumbling to Lucy about flirting with the help.

After what felt like an eternity, Michael finally stepped into the restaurant, his senses immediately overwhelmed. Warmth. The swish of polyester. The mingling scent of coffee and bacon. Voices—unmodulated and unabashed. And color. Everywhere. The interior had been transformed into Santa's workshop.

Employees dressed in elf hats and striped shirts scurried about, helping holiday shoppers. Michael couldn't recall another time in his life when he'd seen so much polyester and so many corduroy jackets adorned with felt elbow patches. With all the polyester-clad seniors shuffling about, he was certain the friction alone could set the place ablaze.

Michael spotted Abraham, standing in the checkout line. He was dressed in a smart-looking gray wool jacket, his black hair styled in a schoolboy part. Michael caught his eye, waved, and worked his way through the crowd to him.

"Last-minute Christmas shopping," Abraham explained, noticing Michael's curious glance at the wooden peg game he placed on the belt.

"I see you're going all out." Michael smiled.

"Secret Santa," Abraham replied. "The gift has to be under fifteen bucks." He held his phone to the credit card console, paid, and scooped up the game. "So, you've got a cup for me?"

Michael nodded. "Yeah. I'm hoping that it still has traces of whatever was used to spike the security guard's drink."

Abraham nodded thoughtfully, listening. "Shall we?" He motioned toward the door.

Michael breathed in the cold air as they stepped outside. A small crowd lingered near the rocking chairs, clutching to-go bags and steaming Styrofoam cups.

"I'm in the black van," said Michael, pointing across the parking lot.

Abraham arched an eyebrow. "Wow," he said, eyeing the van. "This explains so much," he teased.

"I'm helping Ellie with a catering gig," Michael said casually. "Then maybe going on a wild kidnapping spree."

"At least you're staying busy." Abraham laughed.

Michael tapped the key fob, unlocking the van. He leaned in and grabbed the plastic evidence bag from the console. "I don't know if it helps," he said, handing it over, "but the cup had a sort of earthy scent—organic."

"Interesting," said Abraham. "I'm guessing you'll want to check for prints as well?"

"That'd be awesome," said Michael. "I really appreciate you doing this on such short notice."

"Not a problem," Abraham replied. "I'm wrapping up a few things before Christmas—and it's slow this time of year—so, perfect timing."

"Oh, one more thing." Michael circled around to the other side of the van, and pulled out a large flat cardboard box, and a coffee. "Some treats from Olivia: donuts, bagels, cinnamon buns, and a hazelnut creme coffee."

"You're supposed to bribe me *first*, then ask for the favors." Abraham laughed.

"I'm still learning the ropes," Michael said with a wink. "Let me walk you to your car— you've got your hands full."

"Nonsense," Abraham replied, slipping the Cracker Barrel game into his coat pocket.

"You sure?" Michael looked uncertain.

"Yep, just hand me the box." He balanced the evidence bag on top. "And then slip the coffee into my hand. Nothing to it. I'd bow, but—"

"No one likes a show-off." Michael grinned.

"Exactly," Abraham replied.

Michael smiled at his friend and gave him a pat on his shoulder. "I have to run… Ellie's got me on an impossible schedule."

"Not a problem, I'll text you with the results."

"Thanks, Abraham." Michael watched him go, wondering *how* he planned to get his keys out of his pocket.

He climbed into the van, and started the engine. Cold air blasted from the vents, sending a shiver through his body. The dash display popped to life. Gene Autry's melodious voice filled the cabin, singing one of Michael's favorite Christmas classics, "Rudolph the Red-Nosed Reindeer."

Michael put the van in reverse, checked the rearview mirror, and eased out of the busy parking lot. It was 11:15—just enough time to get back to the café, reload the van, and make it to the set before lunch.

Chapter 35

Alexis's eyes lit up when Neil looked up from his script and gave her what she considered the most adorable smile *ever*. He high-fived fellow actor Ian Stewart and strode over to the craft service table.

"Would you accompany me on a tour, my fine lady?" He took Alexis's hand in his and kissed it gently.

"Yes, my lord." Alexis laughed at his silliness, curtsying. She stole a quick glance at Ellie, who gave her a quick smile and then hurried around the table to join Neil.

"I'll show you around the set first," said Neil. He guided her through the maze of cables and lights, pointing things out along the way.

"That's sound, don't trip over their cords—they take it personally. Props is over there, and that's where we pretend to eat actual food."

Alexis blinked, surprised. "You mean you don't actually eat it?"

"Trust me, you wouldn't either. The gravy's been microwaved more times than my career,"

Neil laughed. "Half the time, it's sprayed with glycerin so it shines on camera."

"That's disgusting." Alexis laughed, wrinkling her nose.

"Movie magic." Neil grinned. He gave a quick wave to Camilla Scott and Dillan Wiles across the set. "Come on, let me introduce you to two of my friends."

The two actresses stood near a bank of set lights, discussing the last scene.

"Are you sure we're not… interrupting them?" Alexis asked, not wanting to intrude.

"Of course not," said Neil, waving away her concern. He waited politely for a break in their conversation, and then stepped forward. "Camilla, Dillan—this is Alexis West."

"We've met," said Camilla. "Though, not formally." Her expression softened. "It's nice to be properly introduced. And by the way"—she touched Alexis's forearm—"my Snowfall Latte? *Perfect*. It was *delightfully decadent*."

Camilla's blue-green eyes sparkled as she spoke.

Alexis found her completely mesmerizing—no wonder the cameras loved her. "Thank you so much," she gushed.

"Nice to meet you," said Dillan, taking Alexis's hand.

"Nice to meet you, too," Alexis replied.

The actress arched an eyebrow and leaned in, narrowing her eyes. "I see you've been holding out on me, huh?"

Alexis's eyes opened wide with surprise. "I'm sorry? I'm not sure what you mean."

Dillan's face broke into a wide easy grin, her perfect teeth on full display. "Why, the Snowfall Latte, of course. I hear it's *all* the rage."

"Oh." Alexis let out a breath, her shoulders relaxing.

"Dillan," Neil said, shaking his head. "*Such an actress*," he teased warmly.

"But seriously"—Dillan lowered her voice playfully—"I want one of those lattes."

"Of course." Alexis grinned. "I'm here to—"

Her reply was cut short by David's sudden appearance on set. "Ms. Scott, a moment, please."

A look of concern flashed across Camilla's face. She turned to Alexis, smiled graciously, uttering a quick apology, then hurried off. Neil and Dillan's eyes followed her across the set.

"Is everything okay?" asked Alexis.

"Of course," Neil said, offering a reassuring smile. "David's always calling emergency huddles. It's probably about the sleigh scene tonight."

Across the room, the producer, Kevin Yale, appeared, talking animatedly with David.

Chavon—Victoria's publicist—trailed behind Kevin. Through the sweeping windows facing the ocean, Gerald zipped past in his golf cart, heading toward the front of the house.

Neil and Dillan exchanged a glance. Even Hollywood's elite couldn't hide the sudden shift in atmosphere.

"I'm sorry, Alexis," said Neil as David waved him over. "We'll have to finish our tour another time."

"Yes, of course." Alexis smiled through her disappointment. "Thank you so much, Neil." She turned to Dillan. "It was wonderful meeting you."

"You as well," Dillan said warmly—then she and Neil hurried toward David, who looked more agitated by the second.

Alexis slipped off the set. Michael had just arrived, and Ellie was helping him at the door as he delivered supplies. A sense of unease lingered—as if the other shoe was about to drop… and it wasn't going to be a Jimmy Choo.

Chapter 36

"I just got a text from Olivia," said Ellie, looking up from her phone. "Victoria's death is all over the news."

"It was bound to happen," said Michael. "The studio had NDAs for everyone here, but there's always a leak—usually from the ME or someone else in the mix."

"Yeah," Ellie agreed. "Especially for someone as famous as Victoria."

"And… in a small town," Michael added. "Probably made a fortune leaking that story to the news."

"So what do you think is going to happen?" Alexis asked, joining the conversation.

"They'll try to quash the rumor mill. I'm sure the studio's PR team has been all over this," said Michael.

"Ahem," Peter coughed.

The trio froze. Peter stood a few feet away, his expression tight. Their faces flushed like kids caught with their hands in the cookie jar. His eyes tracked from their faces, settling on their phones.

"So," he said evenly. "I'm sure you've seen the news."

"My associate just texted," Ellie confirmed in a quiet voice. She slipped her phone into her pocket, taking in a calming breath. "I'm sorry, Peter. I know this adds yet another layer of stress to your job."

"It comes with the territory," Peter replied, his tone controlled. "I'll remind you"—his eyes briefly settled on each person—"that you are under strict NDAs."

"Peter, I assure you, you don't have to worry about us," said Ellie earnestly.

"We won't breathe a word," said Michael.

"We're here to help any way we can," added Ellie.

"About that," said Peter, his tone softening.

Ellie's heart dropped. *Are they about to close production?*

"Kevin Yale—the producer—wants to lock down the set."

"Lock down?" Ellie couldn't hide her disappointment. "What does that mean?"

"Kevin wants to limit access to the set," Peter explained. "No new vendors, no outside deliveries—just the essential crew." He hesitated, meeting Ellie's eyes. "I realize this isn't part of your original contract, but Kevin asked if you could handle dinner service for the next few days. You'll be fully compensated, of course."

"Yes!" Ellie exclaimed. "But… without time to fully prepare—tonight would have to be somewhat simple…"

Peter raised his hands. "That's completely fine. I know this came out of nowhere. We've been working with several local restaurants, but Kevin doesn't want any new faces coming in. Security's tightening up too."

"I'll get with Olivia immediately, and start prepping dinner. If you have a menu—perhaps what the stars would like, I can—"

"Already in your inbox." Peter's expression softened. "It's been one of those days. I apologize if I came on a little strong."

"No need to apologize," said Ellie with a kind smile.

"Here," Alexis chimed in. She handed Peter his favorite macchiato and a smaller cup beside it.

"I must have been horrible." Peter laughed. "Two coffees?"

"Not at all," Alexis assured him. "The small one is a Snowfall Latte," she added with a grin. "Camilla's favorite drink, she reminded him. It's becoming quite popular."

Peter took a sip and closed his eyes. "Oh yes." He sighed, taking a sip. "That's heavenly."

Alexis beamed brightly, happy to see her favorite AAD smiling again.

"Perhaps you'd like to partake of one of my buns?" Michael offered.

Peter hesitated, his eyes flicking to the bold lettering on Michael's apron.

"I sense your hesitation." With the flourish of a magician, Michael revealed a pan of freshly baked, gooey-topped cinnamon buns. Decadent swirls of sugary smoke curled into the air.

Peter let out a defeated sigh. "I shouldn't… but sure."

"Careful," Michael warned with a wink. "They're sticky."

"I've been forewarned." Peter chuckled. He finished the latte, and sat the empty cup on the table. "Thank you." He smiled, scooping up the cinnamon bun. "You've helped make an impossible day possible."

Peter turned to leave, then paused. "Ellie, just a quick reminder. We're shooting the sleigh scene outdoors tonight. Please make sure we have hot food ready—perhaps soup—and an abundance of coffee, it would be *greatly* appreciated."

"We'll make it happen," Ellie promised, her voice filled with confidence.

Peter gave a sharp nod. "Twenty-seven degrees tonight," he called as he walked away. "Twenty-seven."

As soon as the mansion doors closed behind him, Michael whipped out a universal remote. He pointed at a small, unassuming door that he had just recently discovered was connected to the sound system, and pressed the plus button. A mischievous smile crept across his face as the room filled with Christmas music.

Ellie shook her head, smiling. It was a fact—Michael West was surely getting coal in his stocking for Christmas.

Chapter 37

The sun's tank was running low as it dipped toward the horizon, painting the sky in shades of pinks and purples. Above the ocean, a pale moon hovered, ghostlike and faint. In a few hours, it would awaken—spilling a shimmering carpet of silver light across the water.

While Alexis and Michael prepped and cleaned, Ellie worked her phone, calling in favors and offering double pay to anyone willing to come in and work the dinner shift at the café. Olivia would join them at the Marlow Mansion while Crystal, the assistant manager, ran the café.

"Dad," said Alexis, motioning Michael over and lowering her voice. "I was just checking Insta—"

"Lexie," Michael said, displeased. "Peter just—"

"No one saw me," she replied, her voice tinged with annoyance. "Listen, there's a story about Camilla being in Lana Cove last week."

"Last week?" Now Michael seemed interested.

"There's tons of pictures. Now that people know, everyone's posting pictures of her around Lana Cove—the grocery store, on the deck of a beach house…"

"Why would Camilla be here… unless—"

"They were going to fire Victoria," offered Alexis.

"Can you email me those pics?" Michael asked.

"Are you sure?" Alexis batted her eyes. "I wouldn't want to do anything… untoward."

Michael was trying to come up with a *réplique qui tue* when his phone buzzed.

Alexis eyed him with mock disdain. "Hypocrite."

"It's Abraham," said Michael. "He's got the results from the cup. I'll be right back."

Michael slipped into the van, the vinyl seat freezing through his pants. Starting the engine, he fished his phone from his pocket. Why didn't he take two seconds to throw on his coat?

A *tap-tap* on the window startled him. It was Gerald. Michael motioned for him to go around the van and get in the passenger seat.

"Perfect timing," said Michael as Gerald climbed in. "Abraham just got the lab results back."

"That's great!" Gerald exclaimed.

Michael jabbed the button for the seat warmer and switched his phone to Bluetooth so Gerald could listen in.

"Hey, Abraham, you've got news?"

"Oh yeah," Abraham said, munching on something crunchy.

"What's he doing—eating a head of lettuce?" Gerald muttered.

"What? Who's that?"

"Sorry, Abraham," said Michael. "You're on speaker. I've got Gerald, the head of security, here with me. He's the one who found the cup."

"Nice to meet you," said Gerald in his gruff sort of way.

"You too," Abraham replied.

"So, you were saying…"

"Right," Abraham continued. "You said it smelled earthy, and you were right. I ran a chemical screen on the residue—the mass spec lit up like a Christmas tree for Kavalactones."

"Of course," said Michael. "Kavalactones. The Flintstones' neighbors."

"You know what he's talking about?" Gerald asked, clearly impressed.

"Not in the slightest," Michael admitted. "Abraham, what are Kavalactones?"

"It's an active compound from kava." Abraham chuckled. "That's what knocked him out. It wouldn't show on a drug test, unless they were looking for it specifically."

"And… it's available to the public?" asked Gerald.

"It is," said Abraham. "You can get kava root at just about any health food store. Highly condensed, it's a potent sedative."

"Seems dangerous," said Gerald.

"A lot of herbs, if misused, are," Abraham agreed.

"Were you able to pull any fingerprints?" asked Michael.

"Yep, clear right-thumb ridge pattern—textbook quality. I've scanned and enhanced it. One minute." Michael could hear the tapping on Abraham's keyboard. "Sending the image to your email now. Should be easy for the department to run through AFIS if they want a match."

A second later, Michael's phone buzzed with an incoming email. Subject line: "PRELIM REPORT – KAVA RESIDUE / DNA / PRINTS."

"I also ran a DNA analysis from the saliva on the rim. I've included that," said Abraham. "It may come in helpful."

"Abraham, you've absolutely outdone yourself. No matter what others say about you, I think you're topnotch!"

"That means a lot coming from you." Abraham chuckled.

"Seriously though, I really appreciate the help," said Michael.

"Of course. Happy to do it," said Abraham, ending the call.

Michael opened Abraham's email and read the report aloud. The evidence was irrefutable—Taylor had been drugged. Abraham went on to say that both kava and alcohol are central nervous system depressants—they slow brain activity, heart rate, and breathing. Combined, the effects multiply, causing loss of consciousness and dangerously shallow breathing.

The report concluded: *The residue detected was a highly concentrated kava root extract—pure, potent and intended to incapacitate.*

Gerald twisted noisily in his seat. "So, Taylor's thermos was spiked with this stuff." He shook his head in disbelief. "He could have died."

"I think whoever did this dosed Taylor just enough to knock him out." Michael's finger tapped the steering wheel to the faint rhythm of "A Holly Jolly Christmas." "I think they're setting up Taylor to take the fall for this—that's why they took his thermos."

"They could take Taylor's blood," Gerald suggested.

"By now, the kava would have metabolized, probably not a trace in his system," said Michael.

"Yeah." Gerald nodded. "It looks bad. Taylor drops her off; he doesn't wait to make sure she gets in her trailer. She fumbles with the lock, passes out, and dies from exposure." Gerald shook his head. "Taylor would have never done that." He thought for a moment. "Now that we can prove Taylor's thermos was spiked, he should be able to get his job back."

Michael hesitated before replying. "Not yet, I wish we could, but—"

"What do you mean?" Gerald's face flushed with anger. "Taylor was drugged." He jabbed a gloved finger at Michael. "It's Christmas, he has a wife and kids. He needs to get back to work."

"I know." Michael raised his hands. "But hear me out," he said, as calmly as possible. "This is an inside job. The thermos is missing; your logbook is missing—*everyone* is a suspect." Michael shifted in his seat, fully facing Gerald. "Right now we have the advantage—no one knows what we've discovered."

Gerald frowned, his eyes meeting Michael's. "I know." His voice was heavy with emotion. "If we say anything, whoever is behind the crime could make it difficult for us."

"Evidence tends to disappear—people begin acting differently," said Michael.

"I did talk with a buddy of mine at the precinct," Gerald confessed.

"About?" Michael's voice was tinged with concern.

"Don't worry, I made sure it didn't sound like I was fishing," said Gerald. "He didn't say much, but they're struggling to come up with enough evidence to rule it as a murder."

"Makes sense," Michael replied. "Right now, they're figuring that she drank too much, got locked out, and froze to death."

"She has a history of showing up on set drunk," said Gerald.

"I remember." Michael nodded. "David even threatened to go to the union because she was in breach of contract."

For a moment, both men sat in silence, lost in their thoughts. From the speakers, the faint, mournful percussion of the "Little Drummer Boy" played softly.

"Gerald, we'll make sure Taylor and his family are taken care of for Christmas," said Michael. "And we'll find out who's behind this and clear his name. I promise."

Gerald gave Michael a long, hard look. "Despite being a pompous jerk… you're a good man."

Michael laughed and patted Gerald's shoulder. "Best compliment anyone's ever given me."

"Well," Gerald said gruffly, "don't get used to it."

Chapter 38

Michael sat alone in the van, using the opportunity to look at the pictures Alexis texted him of Camilla, undisturbed.

The first was a CCTV grab from Preston's—a high-end organic market that smelled faintly like a stable. Camilla, basket in hand, wore a silk scarf, cat-eye thick-framed black sunglasses, and a white Dior wool trench. If she was trying to stay incognito, she was doing a terrible job. The timestamp on the photo revealed it had been taken seven days earlier.

"Hm," Michael muttered, turning his seat warmer to low. *So, Camilla was here a week ago.*

The next text was an Instagram link. Michael tapped it, and Camilla's face filled the screen. The caption read: *Everything that's wrong with Hollywood.* The video cut to a montage of unflattering pictures of Victoria—passed out drunk, her eyes half-open, makeup smeared. It had been viewed nearly ten million times, with over seven million likes.

Michael's stomach twisted. He liked Camilla. And while Victoria had been… well, difficult… this felt beneath her. Cruel. Not like the woman he'd met just a few hours ago.

Alexis's next text was a series of pictures taken from the vantage point of the sea. "Drone," Michael muttered.

The first photo was taken from quite some distance. It showed an expansive three-story beach house, a dusting of snow clinging to its roof. A multi-level deck jutted from the back, connected to a wooden walkway that led to an enclosed pier. Two jet skis sat on raised platforms beside it.

The next picture was much more revealing. The drone's high-powered camera had captured Camilla and a man in what appeared to be a private meeting inside her Florida room.

Camilla Scott was stretched out on a cushioned chaise, a sheaf of papers in one hand, a glass of white wine in the other. Her golden hair was gathered in a stylishly tousled knot atop her head. She was the picture of effortless glamour, in an ivory knit dress, paired with thick gray wool socks—a beauty in repose.

Across from her sat an unidentified man in a collared shirt, layered beneath a cashmere sweater and jeans, his back turned to the camera. One arm was outstretched as if emphasizing a point, the other gesturing midair. The two appeared to be deep in conversation.

Michael stared at the picture.

Why was Camilla in Lana Cove?

Who was she with?

The next shot caught the couple's reaction—the drone's reflection faintly visible in the window. Camilla was on her feet, pointing, the man already hurrying toward the interior of the house.

The final shot, banked up and over the property, revealing the circular drive below. A black Range Rover and Mustang sat parked end to end.

The pictures had been posted three days ago, by someone using the handle *hollywoodskoop*.

Michael swiped back to the picture with Camilla and the unknown man. He zoomed in, but the picture became more grainy as he magnified it. Maybe Alexis knew some way to enhance it without all the degradation.

Deep in thought, he startled when Ellie's face appeared at his window. Michael cut the engine, unbuckled, and climbed out.

"You get lost?" asked Ellie, slightly annoyed.

"Sorry," Michael apologized.

She motioned for him to follow her back to the mansion.

"Abraham sent the results over," said Michael quietly as they stepped inside.

"And?" asked Ellie.

Michael rubbed his hands together. "Abraham said Taylor's cup had residue from highly concentrated kava," he said quietly. "Powerful enough to knock you out. If combined with alcohol, it can be deadly."

Ellie nodded thoughtfully. "So… when are you planning to tell Detective Adams?"

"I'm working on it," said Michael. "Along with a few other things."

Ellie was clearly displeased by his answer, but was distracted by her phone. She glanced at the screen, tapped out a quick reply, and said casually, "Peter."

"Wait—Peter is texting you now?" Michael blurted. "He has your cell number?"

Ellie blinked, surprised by his tone. "We thought it best since Bitter Sweet Café is exclusively providing meals for the shoot."

"Well, what did he want?" Michael asked—sharper than he meant to.

Ellie paused, taking a beat before answering. "He wanted to let me know that they would be rehearsing the sleigh scene from three to seven—oceanfront."

"Oceanfront?" Michael frowned. "It's freezing. Can't they use CGI or something?"

"They're setting up a production tent with industrial warmers," Ellie explained. "Like the ones we use on the café deck. Our job is to keep them well stocked with hot drinks during the rehearsal—and then serve a hot meal afterward." She gave Michael a tired smile, studying his face. "You okay? You seem a bit off."

"I'm fine," Michael replied a little too quickly. "Just tired."

Ellie's phone rang before the conversation could continue. She glanced at the screen and gave him an apologetic look. "I've gotta take this—it's Peter."

"Of course." Michael nodded, fighting back the feeling of jealousy creeping up his spine. He turned away, watching Alexis, who was busily pouring ingredients into a silver mixing bowl. For a moment, she was eight years old again, making cupcakes for school, goopy batter all over the counter and the stove. Now, she had grown into a beautiful woman, befriended by Neil, a Hollywood heartthrob… and Ellie? Ellie has Peter calling her. Sophisticated, handsome, perfect jawline… And who was he stuck with? Gerald.

Behind him, Ellie finished her call. He could hear her hurried footsteps approaching and then her voice. "Can you pick up Olivia at four?" she asked. "We're running low on coffee and mixers for the rehearsal shoot. She's got everything prepped."

"Will do," Michael replied. He moved beside Alexis, who was bent over a bowl, whipping a cinnamon glaze into a caramel-colored froth. "Smells incredible."

Alexis looked up and grinned—she was wearing his apron. Michael couldn't remember the last time he'd been prouder.

"Ellie's teaching me how to make her mom's secret coffee cake."

"Woah!" Michael exclaimed, genuinely impressed. "That's a big deal. She's very protective of her mom's recipes."

"And I'm going to make her proud," said Alexis, cracking an egg neatly against the bowl.

"I know you will." He waited a beat. "Before you start blending again, can I ask a question?"

"Sure, but make it quick," said Alexis. "I need to focus."

Michael pulled out his phone and swiped to the photo of Camilla and the mysterious man. "Is there any way you can zoom in on this—"

"You just move your fingers apart," Alexis said dryly, demonstrating with her forefinger and thumb.

"No, it becomes grainy when I do that—see?" He turned the screen toward her.

"Then just use AI," Alexis said without looking up.

Michael's eyes glazed over. "That's like telling me to *just* perform open-heart surgery."

"Dad…" Alexis sighed, tsking softly. "I'll do it for you after I finish these coffee cakes."

"Thank you, Lexie." He gave her a quick side hug, which she immediately shrugged off.

"Genius at work here," she warned, brandishing a goopy blender. "Famous recipe, so back off."

"Backing off," said Michael, his hands raised in surrender. "I'm going to head out," he told Ellie. "I'll be back in a flash."

"Sounds good," Ellie muttered, tapping away on her tablet.

Michael trudged out into the cold toward the van, beginning to feel more like a pack mule than a man. A team of workers scurried about the shoreline, setting up a massive tent against the biting wind. Another team was laying down some sort of track. Michael winced on their behalf—they had to be freezing.

The van door groaned in protest as he pulled it open and climbed inside. He shut the door and started the engine—his mind was still on the photos.

He shifted toward reverse when an idea struck.

Michael dug out his phone, synced it to the van's Bluetooth and fired off a quick text to Alexis.

Sorry for the text, I know you're busy. Smiley face. Heart. Can you also put the picture with the Mustang in AI? I want to see if it can zoom in on the license plate. Thank you, Lexie. Love you. Heart. Heart. Smiley face.

A moment later, the dashboard display dinged, displaying a thumbs-up emoji.

"That's it?" Michael frowned at the screen. "No heart? No *I love you too?*"

He sank back against the headrest with a sigh, feeling slightly ridiculous for caring—but caring anyway.

I love you too flashed across the display.

Michael took a deep breath, and closed his eyes, feeling her words penetrating through his skin to his heart. *I needed that.*

Chapter 39

The sun hung low on the horizon, a dollop of pink paint smudged across a pale blue canvas. Thin wispy cirrus clouds stretched across the sky, their edges glowing faintly in the fading light. The ocean shimmered like a living painting, as if an artist had dipped their brush into the restless water, blending tendrils of violet and rose with the deep gray of the sea.

"This is beautiful," said Olivia as she climbed out of the van.

"I prefer 'you're beautiful,' but I'll take what I can get." Michael grinned, puffing up his chest.

"Not you." Olivia gave him a playful shove. She turned in a slow circle, taking in the mansion and the snow-covered shoreline. "Well, that kind of ruins the vista," she said, nodding toward Victoria's trailer.

"Not a fan of bright yellow police tape?"

"More of a taupe or mint green girl myself." Olivia smiled.

"Uh-huh. I'm going to start unloading," said Michael. "Gerald,"—he jerked a thumb toward the rotund security guard hustling over—"will give you your security badge. And if you ask nicely, he might even wave his wand over you."

"Michael West!" Olivia pointed a stern finger at him. "Behave."

"What?" Michael shrugged innocently. "It's for security reasons—at least that's what he *told* me."

"Gerald!" Olivia grinned as the man trundled over, his boots clomping, a puff of cold air rolling from his mouth like steam from a locomotive.

"Good afternoon, Olivia." Gerald's gruff voice was the perfect antithesis to his warm smile. "Here's your security badge. Like I told the others—don't lose it, and always keep it visible."

Olivia inspected the badge, then pinned it to her winter coat. "Thank you, Gerald."

"You're welcome," he said with a nod.

"I've gone over everything with her," said Michael as he loaded the hand truck. "She's good to go."

Gerald nodded, though he seemed distracted—shifting from foot to foot. "When you get a chance," he said softly, nodding his head toward the security office.

"Will do," said Michael, curious about Gerald's odd behavior.

Gerald eyed the back of the van, and then turned to Michael. "I'll leave you to it."

Olivia bumped her shoulder against Michael and laughed. "Sounds like you've got a date."

"Sadly, I think you're right," Michael agreed.

"Oh, and do mind his wand," she snickered. "I hear it beeps."

"Close the door behind you," Gerald said, motioning Michael into the tiny security office.

"Are you sure?" Michael asked, squeezing inside. "It's like a glorified closet in here."

Gerald ignored the comment and handed Michael a slightly squished chocolate snowman from his ever-melting stash of holiday treats.

"Thanks," said Michael. "I'll enjoy it later."

"Look," said Gerald, waving Michael's comment aside. "I've only got a few minutes before I meet with the UPM—Unit Production Manager. They're packing and moving Victoria's trailer."

"Moving her trailer?" Michael's face fell. "Can they do that? Isn't it still a crime scene?"

"CSU is done, and the police have released it," said Gerald. "David made it clear he wants the trailer off his set by tomorrow morning."

"Why the hurry?"

"According to the crew," Gerald said, "morale. And the fact that it's smack in the way of some of the outdoor shots."

"I guess." Michael nodded slowly. "Seeing her trailer every day…" His voice trailed off. "It's unfortunate." He sighed. "I really wanted to do a little… exploring."

"Exactly." Gerald's eyes brightened. "It's why I needed to talk to you. The UPM wants me to oversee the team packing up Victoria's belongings."

Michael leaned back against the wall, his shoulder hitting the light switch, plunging the tiny office into darkness.

"Sorry," he muttered, running his hands blindly across the wall. "Where is it?"

"I'll do it," Gerald grumbled, awkwardly pressing against Michael in the pitch-black room.

"I can feel your breath on my face," Michael groaned.

"Move your hand!" said Gerald.

"Where?"

"Just—hold still," Gerald snapped as their coats scraped loudly against each other.

"At least buy me dinner first," Michael muttered.

A beat later, the lights flicked back on with a bright click. Gerald retreated quickly to the middle of the room.

"Sorry," Michael repeated. "Can we move on? I'd like to forget this ever happened."

"Please," Gerald huffed. "For both of our sakes."

"So," said Michael, straightening his coat. "About Victoria's trailer, do you think you can get me in before they box everything up? The police may have missed something—especially if they're leaning toward accidental death."

"That was my plan," said Gerald. "Once rehearsal starts, everyone will be focused on the shoot. It'll be dark—probably best to do it then."

"Sounds perfect to—" Michael's phone buzzed loudly in his coat pocket.

Gerald shot him a suspicious look. "Aw, come on, man…"

"It's my phone," said Michael, fishing it out. "One second."

He slipped off his glove, opened his email, and tapped the attachments. "I asked Alexis to clean up a couple photos for me." He angled the screen so Gerald could see.

"That's Camilla Scott," said Gerald. "How did she get these?"

"Various social media sites," Michael said. "It appears that Camilla's been in Lana Cove for at least a week."

"And no one noticed?" Gerald looked unconvinced.

"She disguised herself whenever she went out in public," he explained. "But," he swiped to the next image. "These drone photos have me a bit confused."

Gerald leaned closer. "What do you mean?"

Michael zoomed in on the frame. "This is Camilla's beach house."

"Yeah…"

"Well… these photos mean someone *knew* Camilla was in Lana Cove and *where* she was staying."

"It would have to be someone on the inside," said Gerald. "One of the bigwigs."

"That's what I think," Michael agreed.

"Any idea who that is with her?"

"No." Michael shook his head. "I was hoping you might recognize him."

Gerald studied the picture more closely. "Sorry—can't tell by the back of his head. But… I have seen that baseball cap before."

"Really?" Michael asked excitedly.

Gerald dragged his sleeve across his nose and cocked his jaw to the side. "Daggett, I can't remember where." He frowned. "Don't worry, it'll come to me."

"Not a problem," said Michael. "What about the papers she's holding. That's a script, right?"

"Yep." Gerald nodded. "When did you say this was taken?"

"Don't know if I did," said Michael. "But the timestamp says seven days ago—a week before Victoria died."

Gerald let out a low whistle. "So she's reading a script a week before Victoria's death."

"Yep," said Michael. He swiped to the next picture. "What about this car? Do you recognize it?"

"Nope," said Gerald. "I've logged every car on set—no one has a black Mustang."

Michael frowned, zooming in a little more. "Alexis used AI to sharpen the image—the plate was blurred before," he explained.

Gerald shook his head, equal parts impressed and horrified. "These kids and their AI."

"I'm pretty sure it's a rental," said Michael. "We find out who rented the car, we find out who our mystery man is."

"How do you know this car is the mystery man's car? He could be driving the Range Rover."

"Because the Mustang doesn't have snow on it; the Range Rover's windshield is still covered, so it hasn't been driven."

"Good point," Gerald agreed.

Michael met Gerald's gaze. "Do you think your buddy on the force could run a plate number for us—quietly?"

"Oh," Gerald muttered. "It's a bit of a big ask."

"But it could blow the case wide open," Michael pressed. "Help us identify the mystery man."

Gerald scratched the bridge of his nose. "Alright, but so you know, my favors-to-value ratio is running a bit thin."

"We're doing this for Taylor," Michael reminded him.

"One more favor," Gerald finally conceded. "That's it though. After that, I'm tapped out."

"Scout's Honor." Michael held up three fingers.

Gerald stared at him, unimpressed. "You were never a scout—and the honor part is questionable."

"Fair," Michael agreed.

Chapter 40

There was a flurry of activity inside the massive production tent as everyone prepared for the upcoming sleigh scene. Portable heaters hummed from every corner, battling the icy wind that blew in from the beach.

Peter marched about the tent, looking like a human Christmas tree—his forest-green puffer jacket was made of stacked circular sections, broad at the bottom, tapering smaller toward the top. Red mittens and black boots completed his ensemble.

"Thirty minutes people," Peter called out through cupped hands.

"This is like organized mayhem," said Olivia from the makeshift café at the rear of the tent.

"It's a well-oiled machine," Michael replied, lining up several stainless-steel dispensers on a long wooden table. Olivia followed behind, setting small cards atop each one: *Coffee, Hot Water, Apple Cider*.

"I'll grab the condiments," said Olivia. "You want to grab the cookies and fruit?"

"Your wish is my command." Michael swooped away, grabbing an oven mitt.

Moments later, the delectable aroma of coffee and freshly baked cookies swept through the tent. Michael arranged chocolate chip and sugar cookies shaped like Santa's head onto circular trays, covering them beneath clear domed lids to keep them warm. Olivia set out milk and creamer.

Michael popped two fresh pans of cookies into the toaster ovens, turned, and froze as the crew suddenly parted.

Camilla swept in, radiant in a red wool coat and a glittering white hat. She waved at Michael as she approached.

"Ms. Scott." Michael smiled, nodding slightly.

"Mister…" Camilla narrowed her eyes and stomped. "Oh shoot!"

"West." Michael laughed, grinning. "The *best* direction."

Olivia watched the playful exchange between the A-lister and Michael, stunned.

"Is that right?" Camilla's eyes roamed over the modest selection of hot beverages. A momentary flash of disappointment appeared and vanished behind a practiced smile.

"The selection's a bit small," said Michael, holding up a finger. "But"—he ducked beneath the table and came up triumphantly with a stainless-steel thermos—"we do have the famous Snowfall Latte and gluten-free gingerbread cookies. Very limited edition."

"You didn't!" Camilla bounced on her toes, delighted.

"An elite professional such as myself *always* thinks ahead," said Michael.

"It was Ellie's idea, wasn't it?" asked Olivia.

"Shh." Michael smiled, waving her comment away.

"Mr. West, you are too sweet," gushed Camilla.

"Thank you." Michael blushed. Camilla's voice was intoxicating—and he was drunk on her words. "Please be careful," he warned, handing her the latte. "It's hot like—"

Don't, Olivia's eyes begged him silently.

"Me."

There it was. Out. No taking it back.

"Gah," Olivia made a strangled noise between a groan and a gag.

Camilla cocked her head, and gave Michael a knowing grin. "Someone's full of themselves." She plucked a cookie from the tray and turned to Olivia. "Keep an eye on this one."

"Sorry," mouthed Olivia, clearly mortified.

Camilla smiled, spun on her heel, and crossed the tent to sit beneath a heater.

"She's absolutely gorgeous," whispered Olivia.

Michael nodded wordlessly as Peter's voice rang out again. "Twenty minutes."

Outside the tent, daylight was quickly fading. The special effects team had transformed the beach into a winter wonderland. Beneath the dusting of artificial snow ran a seventy-foot track, built to guide a modified sleigh whose hidden wheels fit neatly into the grooves— giving it the magical appearance of gliding across the frozen shoreline.

Two midnight-black Friesians stood hitched to the sleigh, their coats gleaming under the lights. A mountain of a man in a top hat and tails kept them calm with apple slices and sugar cubes. Their breath rose in soft, white plumes that drifted into the cold night air.

Michael and Olivia watched from the tent's opening along with several crew members.

Ian and Camilla spoke animatedly with David for a moment, and then walked hand in hand to the sleigh. A small set of wooden stairs had been placed alongside so they could easily climb inside. The man wearing the top hat and tails was already positioned at the reins.

David and Noah stood behind a portable setup, consisting of a row of monitors displaying multiple cameras, glowing blue in the dim light. David tapped his headphones, then spoke into the mic, his voice rang out from the mounted speakers.

"Alright, people—quiet on set."

Instantly, the chatter died away. Only the wind and the rhythmic thrum of generators remained.

Noah made a few last-second adjustments, then nodded.

"Pictures up… and action," David called.

The driver flicked the reins. "Yah!" The Friesians tossed their heads as they began to move, hooves striking the snow-dusted track in perfect unison. White flakes drifted from the snow machines, clinging to their manes as a mechanical camera and drone followed alongside.

Camilla turned to Ian, her laughter filled the air. Ian pulled her close, whispering into her ear. She wrapped him up in a kiss as the horses proudly marched forward, pulling the sled effortlessly. Magic.

"Reset!" David's amplified voice cut through the applause and night air. "We'll go again after review."

Olivia turned to Michael, her eyes bright, filled with wonderment. "This is amazing," she whispered.

Michael smiled back, wrapping his friend in a hug. Christmas had a way of bringing out the child in everyone.

Chapter 41

Michael hurried back to the craft service table, just in time to pull another batch of cookies from the toaster oven. He grabbed a mitt, slid the pan out, and shook the golden brown cookies onto the serving tray.

Unable to resist, he scooped one up, waved it in the air to cool it, and then sank his teeth into the piping-hot sugary sweet. He eyed the pan, his stomach growling—he could easily devour the entire batch.

Olivia must have read his mind because she quickly snapped the domed lid over the tray. "You'll thank me later," she said with a grin.

He was about to reply when his phone buzzed.

Meet me at Victoria's trailer in five.

"Gerald's ready," Michael told Olivia, firing off a quick thumbs-up before pocketing his phone. "I should be back in fifteen."

"Things have calmed down," said Olivia, her eyes roaming about the nearly empty tent. "I'll be fine. If I need you, I'll text." She gave him a worried look. "Don't get caught!"

"Trust me," said Michael, zipping his coat. "I'm more afraid of what Ellie would do to me than anyone else."

"You should be." Olivia watched as he crossed the tent.

Michael turned at the flap, gave her a quick wave, and slipped outside.

If Michael was worried about being seen, he needn't have been. Everyone's attention was glued to the set, and the hum of the generators and roar of the ocean masked the sound of his footsteps.

Still, he played it safe. He hurried to the back of the tent and crouched, hidden in the shadows. He shivered as the cold wind swirled around him, biting through his coat.

Michael didn't have to wait long before the dark silhouette of the golf cart appeared. It rocked from side to side over the uneven icy terrain, the headlights bouncing like two googly eyes. Then with a squeak and a flash of red brake lights, Gerald rolled to a stop in front of Victoria's trailer.

Michael peeked around the corner of the tent. The coast was clear. He slipped out, boots crunching softly, and hurried along a stretch of snowy shoreline. He ducked under a railing and joined Gerald at the golf cart.

Gerald looked around nervously, his breath puffing white in the cold. "Wait here until I get the door open," he whispered. "Then I'll wave you over."

"Got it," Michael replied.

Gerald trudged toward the trailer, his heavy boots thudding against the icy stairs. He pulled a small flashlight from his pocket and shone it on the door. There was a jingling of keys, a soft metallic click, and then the door creaked open. Gerald leaned halfway inside and motioned Michael to join him.

Michael darted across the snow and hurried up the steps. Once inside, Gerald closed the door, twisting the handle to make sure it locked. He pressed a glowing switch, flooding the trailer with light.

"Good Lord," Michael breathed, letting his eyes explore the trailer. The interior was stunning, like a luxury apartment. Polished marble counters, plush furnishings, and gold accents gleamed beneath recessed lighting.

"It's like a luxury condo on wheels," Michael muttered, taking it in.

Gerald gave a small grunt, unfazed by the opulence. "Different life." He pulled a pair of latex gloves from his pocket and handed them over.

"Now we're official," said Michael, snapping them on.

"If you find anything, put it in one of these." Gerald set a stack of plastic baggies on the counter.

Michael nodded. "I'll start with the kitchen."

The counters were mostly clear. Faint circular stains marked where glasses and bottles had once stood. He opened the refrigerator—empty, wiped spotless. *Makes sense*, he thought. *The police probably took anything edible to test.*

Across the room, Gerald searched through a row of sleek black cabinets that lined the wall above a white leather sofa. They too were empty. With a grunt, he turned his attention to the sofa, yanking off the cushions, digging his fingers into every crack and crevice.

"I'm beginning to wonder if she actually lived here," said Michael.

Gerald merely grunted, still on all fours, digging away at the back of the sofa like he was looking for lost change.

Michael removed the top of a domed silver trash can and lifted the bag. Empty—except for a soggy receipt stuck to the bottom. He peeled it free and squinted at the smeared print.

"Gerald." Michael's voice rose. "I found a receipt from a bar called Oliver's. It's timestamped 12:37 a.m.—the night she died."

Gerald rolled to his feet with a groan and joined him. "Oliver's." He nodded. "I know the place. She could go there and have a drink—no one would bother her."

"It's a pool hall, right? Kinda seedy."

"I'll say," Gerald replied. "Oliver Junior runs it now—nasty piece of work. Keeps a private card game in the back. His old man had dirt on half the town, so the police tend to look the other way."

"I'm guessing that they won't have CCTV there either," said Michael.

Gerald barked a laugh. "No, not a chance."

"Think anyone there would talk to us?" Michael asked, already anticipating the look on Gerald's face. "Maybe if I offered them a little, you know, *incentive*?"

"Money talks." Gerald nodded. "But it's a tough crowd."

"Worse than the beachcombers?"

"Yeah," Gerald smirked. "They're more like the gravediggers."

"Great," Michael muttered. "Maybe you should go."

"I'm no longer welcome there," said Gerald flatly. "And before you ask—it's none of your business, and it's a long story."

"And you'd have to kill me," Michael quipped.

An evil grin spread across Gerald's face. "The thought has crossed my mind."

"I tend to have that effect on people," said Michael. He slipped his phone from his pocket, snapped a few pictures of the receipt, and then sealed it in a bag.

Gerald had moved on to the living area, grunting as he manhandled another sofa. Michael explored the other wall where an electric fireplace flickered beneath a widescreen television. In front of it sat a white lacquered teardrop-shaped table; a small army of remotes sat atop.

"At least we know she didn't burn any evidence in the fire," said Michael.

Gerald continued rummaging, ignoring him.

"It's electric…"

No reply.

Michael's attention shifted to a pair of sleek black doors with golden handles. He opened the first, revealing a compact but elegant bathroom—sink, toilet, and a glass-doored shower. Shelves lined the vanity, packed with colorful tubes and bottles of all shapes and sizes.

"*La Mer* moisturizing cream," Michael read aloud with an exaggerated French accent. "Augustinus Bader face oil." He ran his finger across a series of bottles, plucking a crystal-cut flacon from the shelf. "Baccarat Rouge 540."

He gave it a cautious spritz on his wrist. The intoxicating sweetness filled the air—instantly taking Michael back to the moment when Victoria had swept into the Dagmeyer Room.

A pink silk robe embroidered with a glittery "V" hung on a hook by the mirror. Michael eyed it with curious wonder. *Focus,* he chastised himself.

He checked the sink's drain—nothing. He moved on to the toilet, lifting its tank lid—clean. Finally, he stepped into the shower. Rows of luxury shampoos gleamed against the black tile: Leonor Greyl Paris, Le Labo Santal 33. A loofah hung from a gold hook. He crouched down; several golden strands of hair had dried around the drain.

When he stepped back into the hall, the bedroom door stood open. Gerald was holding Victoria's coat, searching through the pockets.

"Where was her coat?" asked Michael.

"Over that chair," said Gerald. "Not tossed, either—carefully laid across the top."

Michael frowned. *If she had been drunk, would she have carefully placed her coat over the chair?* And as Gerald said earlier, if she'd went outside to smoke, she would have put it on. He glanced up; sure enough, there was a smoke detector—just like Gerald had said—over her bed.

Gerald removed a pack of Davidoff Gold cigarettes from her pocket and a slim silver lighter. He dropped them in an evidence bag and set it on the bed.

"Fancy smokes. Did anyone ever find her phone?" Michael asked.

"I'm not sure," said Gerald. "I remember Detective Adams asking about it."

"If she went outside to smoke, I doubt she'd take it with her," Michael reasoned.

"If she'd had her phone, they would have found it outside, along with her."

"And, she would have called someone to come help her," said Michael. "I'll ask Detective Adams if they found her phone. If not… it means the killer most likely took it."

"Meaning there was most likely something on there they didn't want anyone to see," Gerald replied.

"Who was it that found her again?"

"Peter," said Gerald.

"That's right." Michael gave a quick nod. He turned his attention to the bed. The sheets were tangled, blankets kicked to one side, and the pillows lay crumpled and shoved away from the headboard. Michael leaned closer, studying one of them. He brought the pillow to his nose and inhaled.

Gerald cocked an eyebrow and gave Michael a concerned look. "Things aren't going to get weird, are they?"

"PI training," Michael explained. "When investigating a crime scene, we learned to use all our senses." He sniffed again. "There's a hint of cologne on this pillow." He turned the pillow over. His eyes widened. "And… a gray hair. *Gerald…*"

"It's not mine, you idiot," growled Gerald.

"Let me smell your cheek," said Michael.

"You touch me and I'll snap your finger in two," Gerald warned.

"As long as it's not my pinky," said Michael. "I need it when I drink my tea." He extended his little finger, pretending to hold a cup.

Gerald gave Michael a hard look.

Michael removed the hair from the pillow and sealed it in a plastic bag. "You know," said Michael, "it's probably Noah's. Doesn't he have gray hair?"

"He's got some gray hair, kind of salt-and-pepper," said Gerald.

"Did you ever see Noah and Victoria together—off set?"

"Not that I recall," said Gerald. "But, like I told you, she was very serious about her privacy."

"We need one of his hairs," said Michael. "Is he staying in the mansion?"

"Yes," said Gerald slowly, not liking where this conversation was heading.

"Then we need to take a peek in his room—see if his cologne matches the pillowcase. I'm sure we can find his hair in a brush or something."

Michael carefully pulled the pillowcase free and set it on the chest of drawers. Then he lowered himself beside the bed, balancing on his hands and knees.

There was a loud, meaty *smack*, followed by a startled yelp. Michael toppled sideways, crashing into the chest of drawers, landing flat on his back.

Chapter 42

Gerald jumped back as a figure dressed in black rolled from beneath the bed. The intruder scrambled to their feet and dashed for the door, but Gerald recovered quickly, moving with surprising speed for someone his size. He leapt through the air and tackled the mysterious stranger to the floor.

Michael staggered to his feet, blood trickling from his nostrils. He stumbled over Gerald's feet, caught his balance, and yanked the knit beanie off their attacker.

"Chavon," he gasped, seeing her raven-black hair.

"Get off me, you behemoth," she growled, twisting and kicking beneath Gerald's weight.

Gerald moaned and slowly climbed to his feet, one heavy hand clamped around Chavon's arm.

Michael snatched two tissues from a box and stuffed one in each nostril to staunch the bleeding.

"What are you doing hiding in the trailer?" Gerald rounded on her.

Chavon whirled on him, kicking him viciously in the shin. Gerald's lips pursed into an "O"; his eyes rolled up in their sockets. Michael winced as somehow Gerald swallowed the pain.

"I'll have your job for this," Chavon spat. "I'm Victoria's assistant, I have every right to be here."

"You're trespassing, and this is a crime scene," Gerald growled. "How did you get in here?" Chavon answered his question with a scowl.

Michael bent down and picked up a large crossbody bag, the strap torn during the scuffle. He flicked open the silver clasp and lifted the flap.

"Give me that." Chavon lunged for him. "You can't look in there!" she shouted, wrestling against Gerald's vicelike grip. "That's private property."

"Look at this," said Michael, pulling out the contents one by one. "Seems like our friend's been busy." He set a heavy gold-plated bottle of Roja Parfums Haute Luxe on the white lacquer table, followed by a diamond-encrusted snowflake brooch, a diamond tennis bracelet, a medicine bottle filled with colorful pills, and finally a Valmont and Company alarm clock.

Michael held it up. "I understand the jewelry and perfume… but why would you steal her alarm clock?"

"I'm not telling you a thing," Chavon snapped defiantly. Her eyes narrowed as she scrutinized Michael's face. "Aren't you that *crafty* guy?"

"I'm undercover," said Michael smugly. "I just happen to be a detective." He crossed his arms, his nose whistling.

"Michael, call Detective Adams," said Gerald. "We're looking at, what—at least a hundred-grand theft?"

"Pretty good motive to want Victoria out of the way," said Michael. "With her gone, she could help herself to her jewelry and perfume."

Chavon's eyes went wild. "Are you *crazy*? I wouldn't hurt Victoria, I loved her."

"You have a strange way of showing it," said Michael. He slipped his phone out of his pocket and started to dial.

"Stop!" Chavon shouted. "What do you want to know?"

"I know you're here to rob Victoria… but I'm curious, why the alarm clock?" asked Michael.

"It has a camera," Chavon snapped.

Michael's finger froze, hovering above the call button. "Go on."

"Victoria was filming *certain* people," Chavon said breathlessly. "Prominent people. She was going to use it to blackmail them."

"Blackmail? Why?" Michael frowned. "She's rich and famous."

"If you hadn't noticed, she's also a troublemaker," said Chavon. "Studios didn't want to deal with her. She was losing roles to younger actresses. So, she began filming… *private* encounters. In her bedroom."

Michael studied the alarm clock; he could see it now, a tiny pinprick above the twelve. "Her killer might be on here," he said quietly.

Chavon's expression hardened. "Killer? Victoria wasn't *killed*, you idiot. She got stoned out of her mind and passed out on the porch."

Michael was tempted to enlighten her with what they had discovered—but stopped himself. "Do you know who she was out with the night she died?" he pressed.

Chavon hesitated, then let out a long sigh. "Look, I have a lot of information—a *lot*. So, how about we make a deal? I answer your questions, and we pretend this little encounter never happened."

Michael glanced at Gerald. Neither of them spoke, but the look said everything—*can we trust her?*

"Trust me." Chavon smiled coolly, as if reading their thoughts. "I know stuff that'll make your toes curl… about everyone."

Michael crossed his arms. "Alright. But if we find out you're lying, the deal's off."

"Oh, there's no need to lie," she purred. "The truth is far juicier than fiction."

"So," said Michael, leveling his gaze. "Back to my earlier question—who was Victoria with the night of her death?"

"I really socked you good," Chavon smirked, admiring her work. "She was with either Peter or Noah."

"Really?" Michael said, not fully convinced. "Neither really seem like Victoria's type."

"They were just pawns," said Chavon with a shrug. "Simply put, they both had something Victoria wanted. After this shoot, Noah's working on a spy thriller with Matt Damon and Chris Hemsworth. They're still looking for a female lead. Noah just happens to be best friends with the director, so Victoria was looking for opportunities."

Michael tilted his head. "So, she was sleeping with him?"

"Of course." Chavon laughed. "Noah was head over heels in love with her. Poor sod."

"And Peter?" asked Michael.

A nasty smile crept across Chavon's lips. "Oh Peter, that naughty boy. All those times he rushed off set in a huff to 'find' Victoria—purely performative. He'd bang on the trailer door, disappear inside—" she let the sentence hang. "I don't think I need to continue."

"Anyone else?" asked Michael.

"I know our first night here, she had a little *tryst* with David."

"With the *director*?" Michael gave her a dubious look.

"Why? Because he's a *family* man?" Chavon pouted, her tone dripping with sarcasm. "As far as I know, it only happened once." Then the wicked smile returned. "Oh how she *loved* to push his buttons on set. They had a love-hate relationship."

"Did Peter and Noah know that she was sleeping with both of them?" asked Gerald.

"Good question," said Chavon. "When you asked who she was with the night of her death, I said Peter or Noah. *Initially*, she went out with Peter—to this swanky bar…" She closed her eyes, searching her memory, tapping her lips with her finger.

"Oliver's?" Michael prompted.

Chavon looked at him like he was an idiot. "I said *swanky*, not a dump. Then again"—she looked Michael up and down—"I understand, you poor thing, you don't look like you get out much."

"Neither will you," Michael shot back, "if you don't start taking this seriously."

"Lighten up—so hostile," Chavon fussed, waving a manicured hand. The gesture caught the light and Michael noticed a diamond-encrusted Rolex on her wrist. *I wonder if she stole that too.*

"It was a little place off of Beach Street," she continued. "The Love and Groove Bar."

"I know the place," said Michael. "Mostly hipsters. Peter would fit right in."

"Exactly," Chavon agreed. "Peter took her there. Somehow, Noah found out. Actually, I had a suspicion that he hid a tracker on her somewhere; he *always* knew where she was."

"Interesting," said Michael. "So Noah shows up at the bar?"

"Yeah, he caught them making out—big fight—Victoria texted me to come clean up the mess. Seems she flipped a glass table, shattering it, and tore some pictures off the wall."

"And you—"

"I go in and smooth everything over with the owner," said Chavon, cutting Gerald off. "In the end, everyone's happy."

"Then what happened?"

"That's when Vic and Noah went to that vile place, Oliver's." Chavon grimaced. "And before you ask, I had a couple of drinks with

Martin—the owner of the Love and Groove Bar—Ubered back here, and went to bed. I didn't know anything had happened to Victoria until Peter found her."

"Did you get any texts or messages from Victoria that night?"

"Crickets," said Chavon with a shrug. "Look, I've answered all of your questions. Can I go?"

Gerald scowled, clearly unhappy about letting her walk away, and even less happy about his throbbing shin. But a deal was a deal, and she was leaving, empty-handed.

"I'll give you a ride back to the mansion," Gerald said stiffly. "You collect your things, and you're out of here by tonight—or I will have you arrested."

"Well, aren't you a gentleman?" Chavon purred, her lips curling into a smile that only infuriated Gerald more. She glanced at Michael and tapped the side of his nose. "You might want to ice that."

With a flick of her wrist, she spun on her heel and strutted toward the front of the trailer, Gerald lumbering after her. Michael stood there, seething.

Chapter 43

Michael peeled off his sweaty latex gloves and pocketed them along with his bloody tissues. He washed his face in the sink and then returned to Victoria's bedroom.

The trailer creaked and groaned as a gust of wind whipped up the shoreline. For a moment, he imagined the trailer breaking free from the foundation—rolling along the icy beach, into the ocean. As long as he floated somewhere warm, where he could lounge in a chair and drink fruity tropical drinks, he'd be fine with it.

He crouched beside Victoria's closet, pushing aside a small mountain of designer handbags when he spotted a Dior tote tucked in the corner. Working quickly, he slipped the folded pillowcase, the baggie with the hair, the digital alarm clock, and the receipt inside.

He exited the bedroom and paused at the bathroom, using the mirror to inspect his throbbing nose—it was red and swollen, much like Rudolph's. At least it didn't glow.

Stuffing the tote bag beneath his jacket, Michael cracked open the front door, and peered into the night. The door shuddered against the force of the wind. Carefully, he maneuvered down the icy steps and crept across the dark shoreline toward the production tent.

He slipped inside just as the sleigh reached the end of the track. A smattering of applause rippled through the crowd. Near the craft service table, a handful of crew members huddled around the coffee dispensers and cookies.

Michael shot Olivia a thumbs-up as he hurried over.

"What happened to your nose?" Olivia asked, brushing a long swirly tendril of hair from her cheek, tucking it behind her ear—a worried look on her face. "And why do you smell… sweet?"

"Baccarat Rouge 540," said Michael, stretching out his arm. "Nice, right?"

"Very."

The coffee dispenser sputtered and gurgled loudly as a crewmember began filling their cup—a sure sign it was nearly empty.

Olivia gave the young man a smile. "Give me one second and I'll refill it." She turned to Michael. "Give me a hand—and then tell me *everything*!"

Olivia replaced the coffee dispenser and set another pot to brew. While she tended to the coffee situation, Michael noticed the cookie trays were nearly empty. He lined a row of fresh cookies onto a pan and slid it into the oven. When he turned back, Olivia was waiting—arms crossed, hip canted forward, an eyebrow cocked. If she were a gun, she'd be locked and loaded.

"Alright, Mr. West. Start with the nose."

Michael told her about the intruder, her purse filled with jewelry and perfume, and how he'd *valiantly* exchanged blows to keep her from escaping. He assured Olivia that Chavon was a black belt in some ancient martial art. She, of course, eyed him with deep skepticism. A while back, Michael had been disarmed of his junior-sized little slugger baseball bat by a woman intruder and then beaten to a pulp with it.

"And in the end, we found this." Michael produced the digital clock with an exaggerated flourish.

"A clock." Olivia looked thoroughly unimpressed—similar to everyone's reaction to their earlier *cup* clue.

"It's a hidden camera," Michael said excitedly.

"Oh, that's creepy," said Olivia. "It's why I refuse to do Airbnb." She shuddered visibly. "Gross."

"Yeah, I'm with you on that one." Michael nodded solemnly. "So, Victoria was filming everyone she slept with—and using the video to blackmail them."

"Why?" Olivia frowned.

"I asked the same thing," said Michael. "Chavon said Victoria was losing roles to younger actresses. And that she stirred up trouble on every set—no one wanted to work with her. The videos were her insurance policy."

"And her payday." Olivia's eyes darkened. "That means she may have dirt on some very powerful people. People who'd kill to keep it quiet."

"I've been thinking about that," said Michael. "But how would they even know they were being filmed? As far as I can tell, Chavon was the only one that knew."

"Maybe Chavon told someone. Maybe Chavon was in on the murder," said Olivia. "You *did* say she was stealing hundreds of thousands of dollars' worth of Victoria's jewelry and perfume."

Michael nodded, thinking. "Maybe Victoria had already started blackmailing people—and that's why she was murdered."

"Could be," Olivia agreed. "Who was she sleeping with?"

"So far, Peter the Assistant Assistant Director; David the director; and Noah the cinematographer. There could be more—we won't know until we see the videos."

"Busy woman," Olivia muttered.

The toaster oven dinged. A fresh batch of cookies was ready. Michael slipped on a mitt and scooped them onto the serving plate.

"Given up on arranging them?" Olivia teased.

"Honestly, I never thought cookies should be orderly." Michael grinned, placing the dome over them. He looked up just as Gerald limped over.

"Are you okay?" asked Olivia, her brow creasing with concern.

"I'll be fine," said Gerald, wincing. "Took one to the shin. I swear," he said, rubbing his shin. "That woman kicks like a mule."

"Michael told me how he took her down," Olivia said. "He's so brave."

"Oh, he did, did he?" Gerald eyed Michael and laughed. "He's a regular Mike Tyson that one." He grabbed a paper cup and filled it generously with coffee. He inhaled deeply, savoring the aroma.

"Have a cookie," offered Michael, "fresh out of the oven."

"Don't mind if I do, *champ*."

Michael lifted the dome and Gerald helped himself to a handful of cookies, casually dropping a few of them into his pocket.

"He does that with soup too," said Michael.

Gerald ignored the dig, took a long sip from his coffee, and leaned in slightly.

"First—this is for you." He dropped a key into Michael's palm.

"First you grope me in your office, and now you give me your room key? You're a great guy and all, but really," Michael deadpanned.

"How you survived with all your teeth, I'll never know," Gerald muttered.

"I've wondered the same thing." Olivia nodded.

"I'm lovable." Michael shrugged.

"Debatable," Olivia countered.

Gerald sighed in exasperation. "The key is a master key, so you can get into Noah's room. I'll text you the exact location. Trust me—the mansion's a maze."

"Are you sure about this? What if somebody sees me?" said Michael.

"No one is going to care. You're in craft services—say you're delivering something." Gerald shrugged.

"Okay." Michael pocketed the key, already imagining a million ways this could go wrong.

A wide grin spread over Gerald's face. "Now, for the *coup de grâce*. My guy at the station came through. The Mustang that was at Camilla's beach house was rented from Hertz to a..." he glanced over his shoulder, then turned back. "Peter Star."

"So, that's Peter in the picture at Camilla's beach house?" Michael gave a low whistle.

"Looks like it." Gerald nodded.

"That means Peter knew—a week before Victoria was murdered—that she was being replaced."

"Yep." Gerald nodded.

"That's cold," said Olivia.

"Good work, Gerald." Michael smiled. He lifted the dome. "Have another cookie."

"Speak of the devil," whispered Olivia. "Peter's heading this way."

Gerald closed his eyes, bracing for a lecture.

Peter approached the table, rubbing his hands together briskly. "It's f-freezing out there," he stammered, his teeth chattering like miniature jackhammers.

"Let's warm you up," said Olivia. She grabbed a cup, filled it, adding a dash of cream and a spoonful of sugar. Michael adjusted the towering heat lamp so it shone directly over him.

"Thank you," Peter muttered. Coffee danced in the cup, sloshing from side to side as his hands trembled. "We're finishing up, so if you'd like to help Ellie, we're going to try for dinner about half an hour early. Ian and Camilla are popsicles."

"I bet," said Michael. "The wind coming off the ocean is brutal."

"Electrical built-in heaters into the sleigh," said Peter, rubbing his arms. "But the windchill's in the single digits."

"That's insane," Olivia sympathized.

"I'll help you guys load up," said Gerald, "and drive you back."

"That would be wonderful," said Olivia. "Thank you."

"No worries," said Gerald, tossing his empty cup into the trash.

"Alright," Peter said, topping off his coffee, his trembling settling down to the occasional spasm. "I'll see you at the mansion."

Michael watched him walk away, looking like a man without a care in the world. Or maybe, like a man who'd just gotten away with murder?

Chapter 44

Michael had barely crossed the threshold into the Dagmeyer Room when Alexis darted toward him, throwing her arms around his shoulders.

"Dad! Ellie's invited us to the café after the dinner—and Neil's going to stop by. Oh my God!"

"I wish you were a little more excited," Michael teased.

"Mind if I squeeze by you two?" Olivia asked from the doorway.

"Sorry," said Michael, shuffling out of the way.

"Can you believe it?" Alexis shook her head, eyes sparkling. "Best Christmas ever—except for the murder, of course," she added solemnly. "But otherwise…" She shrugged.

Michael chuckled. "I get it," he said, his heart swelling with his daughter's happiness. "I'm so happy for you."

He hung up his coat, and followed her to the craft service table, where Ellie was putting the final touches on the meal.

"I borrowed some decorations from around the room," Ellie said with a devilish grin. She gestured to a beautiful poinsettia arrangement and slender red candles dusted with gold.

"It's beautiful," said Michael. He stole a quick glance at the *warrior in repose* statue—relieved his strategically placed fig leaf was still attached.

Ellie caught his look. "Oh, don't worry," she said playfully. "I didn't want you to feel jealous."

"Ha!" Michael scoffed. "As if."

Olivia watched the exchange, arms crossed, an amused look on her face.

"Please," Alexis begged, groaning. "*Any* other topic. *Anything*. I had to suffer through Art Appreciation in college. *So* many statues."

"That was an abysmal class," said Michael.

"Not as abysmal as this conversation," Alexis muttered, returning to her bowl and whisking a homemade salad dressing.

"Ellie," said Michael, walking along the table toward her. "I need to slip out for a minute."

"Okay," she said over her shoulder, setting a gleaming silver chafing tray on the table. "How long—" Ellie's eyes widened. "What happened to your nose?"

"Oh that," Michael said casually, shrugging. "Chavon punched me."

"She *punched* you?" Ellie gasped, horrified. Alexis stopped stirring and stared.

"It's nothing," Michael insisted.

"Nothing," Ellie repeated, incredulous. "Have you seen your nose?"

"In passing," said Michael nonchalantly. He lowered his gaze, crossing his eyes to inspect it. "Hm. Now that you mention it, it is a little swollen."

Alexis handed him a folded napkin. "I put some ice inside."

"Thank you—"

"For God's sake, Michael," Ellie interrupted. "Why did Chavon punch you?"

"She was hiding under the bed—I startled her, and she punched me in the face—"

"*Whose* bed?" Ellie interrupted sharply. "Why were you in a bedroom with Chavon?" Michael took a step back. Ellie's face reddened like a thermometer in July—growing redder by the second.

"Wait," Michael said quickly, holding up his hands. "Whatever you're thinking, I can assure you—"

Olivia stepped forward and placed a calming hand on Ellie's shoulder. "Maybe you should let me explain."

"Yes, please." Michael motioned for her to continue.

"Chavon was hiding in Victoria's bedroom," Olivia explained. "She was trying to steal her belongings. Our beloved hero Michael… apprehended her."

"*Bravely*," Michael added.

"*Bravely*," Olivia echoed, choking back a laugh.

Ellie's expression softened, the color faded from her cheeks. "Why didn't you just say that?" She punched Michael in the shoulder.

"Sorry," said Michael, even though he wasn't quite sure what for. "Full confession later, I promise." He shifted on his feet, glancing toward the door. "But right now, I've *got* to get to Noah's room before he gets back."

"Is he a suspect?" Ellie's eyes widened.

Michael gave a tight nod. "Gerald's stalling him as long as possible so I can poke around in his room."

"There's no way Noah could have done such a thing," said Ellie. "He gives off serious bohemian vibes."

"I agree," said Alexis. "He wears Birkenstocks without socks. No self-respecting criminal does that."

Michael's mouth twitched into a smile, she was clearly his daughter. "Good point." He looked from Alexis to Ellie. "If Noah shows up before I'm back, text me."

"I will," said Ellie, nodding quickly.

Michael grabbed a cup of coffee and a paper bag—part of his guise of delivering food—and then headed toward the imposing twelve-foot doors that separated the Dagmeyer Room from the mansion. Thanks to Gerald, he knew Noah's room was up the central staircase, directly off the main hall.

Michael pushed through the heavy doors and stepped into the mansion proper. He paused as the doors closed behind him with a soft metallic click. The word *opulence* came to mind—not whispered, but shouted. It was as if each magniloquent item had been meticulously ticked off who's-who list of pretentiousness.

Variegated, shimmering white marble floor—check. Golden sconces with towering candles—check. Oil paintings of severe men and women in gilded frames—check. Classical music floating through the air softly mingling with the faint scent of vanilla and cinnamon—check. Suit of armor? No, well, one couldn't be too ostentatious.

Thankfully, the halls were empty. Michael shifted the scalding hot coffee to his other hand, wishing he'd grabbed a sleeve. As he moved forward, the hallway opened into a grand foyer. To his right, a sweeping staircase curved upward—golden railings, crimson carpet running down the middle, cedar garlands wrapped in tiny golden lights.

The staircase reminded him of *Gone With the Wind*—the 1940s classic starring Clark Gable and Vivien Leigh. A flash of memory: Scarlett's doomed tumble down the stairs, symbolizing her fall from pride and control to vulnerability.

He shifted the coffee once more, and started to climb the stairs. At the top, Michael came to a wide balcony overlooking the grand foyer. A polished wooden railing ran along the edge, supported by hand-carved balusters. He leaned over the railing, gazing down at an enormous Christmas tree, glittering with crystal ornaments and white lights. Candles flickered in tall windows, and a chandelier scattered diamonds of light across the marble below.

Against his better judgment, Michael set the bag and cup on the floor and snapped a few selfies. His justification? They would look fantastic on his social media feed and the inside flap of his future bestseller. *Always best to be prepared.*

He crossed the balcony and stopped in front of the first door, *The Pelican Suite*. A red *Do Not Disturb* sign hung from the golden doorknob. The door itself was a thing of beauty—carved with intricate inlays and delicate scrollwork. Michael stole one last glance down the hall, sat the coffee on the floor, and unlocked the door using Gerald's master key.

Once inside, he made sure the door was locked behind him and waited a moment for his eyes to adjust. He found the light switch and flicked it on. A familiar scent filled the air—the same fragrance from Victoria's pillowcase. Noah's cologne.

Like everything else in the mansion, the room was stunning. Michael set the coffee and bag on Noah's nightstand, turned, and faced the room.

A California-king four-poster bed dominated the back wall. Half a dozen silk pillows lay scattered like islands in a twisted sea of sheets and blankets. Either Noah was a very active sleeper… or he'd had company last night.

Two mahogany desks stood on opposite sides of the room, cluttered with papers, notebooks, and expensive-looking camera gear. A pair of high-backed chairs faced a massive flatscreen mounted on the far wall. The crimson carpet underfoot was so thick it muffled his steps completely.

Michael continued across the room through a doorway on the right; it led to a second room, equally lavish. Two velvet sofas and several deep armchairs encircled a low glass table. An empty bottle of Opus One 2018 and two glasses sat atop the table, confirming Michael's suspicion that Noah had a visitor.

He scooped up a wine glass. A faint crescent of lipstick clung to the rim. Michael zoomed in, with his phone and snapped a photo. His phone vibrated, startling him.

A text from Gerald: *About to drive Noah and David back now.*

Michael's pulse quickened. He tapped out a quick reply. *Got it!*

He hurried across the room to the bathroom, flipped the light switch, and blinked as brilliant white lights flooded the space—gleaming like a spa. Marble tiles covered the walls and floor. A long mirror stretched across the wall above a double-basin porcelain sink.

"Hair and cologne," Michael reminded himself of his mission.

Noah's tortoiseshell hairbrush was easy to find. Michael slipped on a latex glove with a snap, pulled a plastic bag from his pocket, and delicately plucked several hairs from the brush—carefully dropping them into the bag and sealing it.

"Hm," said Michael, picking up a prescription bottle, reading the label aloud. "Propecia." Setting it down, he began searching through a panoply of facial creams, bronzers, and collagen serum.

"Aha," he exclaimed softly, spotting a dark glass bottle of Tom Ford's Oud Wood. He lifted it to his nose and inhaled, recognizing the scent immediately. "You dirty dog."

He plucked a tissue from a black dispenser, dabbed it with cologne, and sealed it in another baggie. He was on a roll—two pieces of evidence down.

Michael made a quick sweep of the rest of the bathroom. Finding nothing of interest, he flicked off the light. As he stepped through the doorway, the glint of a stainless-steel mini-fridge tucked beneath a countertop and sink caught his eye. He knew he should go, but curiosity got the better of him.

He knelt and opened the door. Inside, bathed in sterile white light, stood a row of tiny glass bottles—umcka, sambucus, ginseng, echinacea, and ashwagandha—lined up like a wellness apothecary.

Michael snapped a quick picture and was about to pocket his phone when it buzzed with a text from Ellie.

Noah's on his way!

Michael shut the refrigerator and bolted for the bedroom. He opened the door cautiously and peeked into the hall. Empty—but he could hear faint voices coming from the bottom of the staircase. He was about to slip out when he remembered: the coffee and the bag. In two strides, he crossed the room and grabbed them from the nightstand.

The voices grew louder—footsteps approaching.

Then the soft, unmistakable click of a key sliding into a lock.

Michael froze. His pulse thundered in his ears.

The doorknob turned. Noah stepped into the room.

Chapter 45

Michael lay spread-eagle beneath the bed. From his narrow view, he could see Noah's feet as he walked about. He stopped, kicked off his shoes, then pressed a socked foot into the carpet, cracking his toes—first one foot, then the other.

Michael's phone vibrated. In the silence, it sounded like a bomber buzzing overhead.

Noah's feet froze. Michael imagined the man's expression: head cocked to the side, searching, listening. A long agonizing minute passed. Finally, Noah shuffled toward the nightstand. A moment later, the television clicked on.

He flicked through the channels, finally stopping at TMZ, the entertainment news channel.

"According to our source," the anchor announced, "Victoria's death may not have been an accident."

"That's right, Lucas," another voice chimed in. "We've confirmed that toxicology reports show high levels of kava in her system."

"Kava," the other host echoed. "Yes, it's an herbal supplement that can be used as a sleep aid—combined with alcohol…"

Michael could see Noah's feet again—moving quickly now, pacing. "Turn on TMZ," Noah barked into his phone, his voice mixed with urgency and fear. "They're saying Victoria was drugged."

Michael held his breath, listening. He could hear the other person's voice, but not clearly enough to distinguish what they were saying.

"Kava," Noah said again. "The herb." The other person spoke again, to which Noah replied, "Okay, I will."

Noah rushed into the other room. Michael heard the refrigerator door wrench open, followed by the sharp clink of glass bottles.

He's getting rid of the evidence.

Noah began speaking again, voice lower but urgent. "Meet me downstairs by the tree. Now." Noah slipped on his shoes. A few seconds later, the door clicked.

Michael didn't hesitate. He slid out from beneath the bed, heart pounding. He grabbed the coffee and the bag and then, sprinting across the room, tore out the door without even bothering to look over his shoulder—taking the stairs two at a time.

Less than a minute later, pale as a ghost, Michael strode across the Dagmeyer Room toward the craft service table—feeling like he might be sick and possibly in need of a fresh pair of underwear.

He looked up and met Ellie's eyes. *He'd made it.*

Chapter 46

It was late when Gerald's ancient SUV rolled to a stop outside the Bitter Sweet Café. He cut the engine, which defiantly continued to chug—finally overcome by a jolting spasm, it shuddered and unceremoniously died.

Michael ended his call with Abraham, and eyed Gerald. "Your car may need resuscitation—perhaps a pastor."

"She just needs someone who understands her," Gerald huffed, patting the cracked dashboard defensively. He twisted in his seat and hit the seatbelt release, letting it fly back unchallenged.

Michael got the message. Gerald was oddly sensitive about his car.

Gerald wiped his nose with his sleeve and eyeballed Michael. "So what did Abraham say?" he asked gruffly.

"He can analyze the hair first thing in the morning," said Michael. "I'm going to have Uber Connect take it to him. Ellie really needs me early tomorrow morning."

"You're kidding me, right?" Gerald snorted. "You're using *Uber* to transport homicide evidence?"

"Crazy, right?" Michael grinned.

"Might as well toss in a breakfast sandwich while you're at it," Gerald smirked.

"You know what," Michael mused, unclasping his seatbelt and pushing open the door. "That's not a bad idea."

Gerald muttered something under his breath.

"Come on," said Michael cheerfully, stepping out into the cold. "They're waiting on us."

"Michael," Ellie called from behind a gleaming glass counter filled with all kinds of tasty treats. "Bring these over to the table." She handed him a six-pack of Maple Run Amber—a local craft ale—and a steaming cup of cinnamon-spiced apple cider for Alexis.

Michael set the hot mug in front of Alexis and distributed the beers around the table. Olivia and Ellie arrived moments later with two oversized plates piled high with warm cinnamon donuts—still glistening with sugar—and a bowl of golden sausage-and-cheese balls—their edges perfectly crisp, a toothpick poking out of each one for easy grabbing.

Gerald's eyes widened with delight. "This is *wonderful*, thank you."

"Of course." Ellie smiled brightly. She passed out several small plates and placed a stack of napkins at the center of the table.

Michael, decidedly not a beer guy, cracked open a Maple Run and took an exploratory sip. "Okay… That's *really* good," he said, pleasantly surprised.

"Better than your appletinis?" Olivia teased.

"Let's not get carried away." Michael grinned.

Gerald didn't wait on the others—he grabbed a donut and several sausage balls, piling them onto his plate. "Sure beats the frozen burrito dinner I was going to eat tonight."

Ellie beamed happily. Gerald may be a little rough around the edges, but he was beginning to grow on her.

"Oh—before I forget." Gerald pushed back from the table and dug into his pocket. He handed each of the women a candy cane, and then turned to Michael. "Here." He placed a Santa Pez dispenser in his hand.

Michael's eyes lit up. "No way—I haven't had one of these since I was a kid." He flipped Santa's head. Empty. The disappointment on his face was palpable.

"Sorry," Gerald grumbled. "I got hungry."

Olivia snorted into her beer as Michael struggled with the appropriate amount of outrage he should express.

Just then, Alexis squealed, nearly sloshing her drink. "Neil will be here in twenty minutes! He's waiting on his Uber."

"That's wonderful," said Michael. "Let's eat all the food before he gets here."

"Dad!" Alexis shot him her patented playfully-furious glare.

"Speaking of Uber," Gerald said through a mouthful of donut. "Michael is using Uber to send murder evidence to the lab."

He watched Ellie and Olivia eagerly to see their reaction.

"What?" said Michael, unfolding his hands, palms turned up as if revealing his cards. "Uber Connect has 4.7 stars on Google. And I can't abandon everyone. I'm *indispensable* at the crafty table—some would say I'm the social glue holding this whole production together."

Ellie coughed, "I'm glad your humility keeps you grounded."

"I think he's been sniffing the social glue," Gerald mumbled.

"Well…" Michael stretched back in his chair, folding his hands behind his head. "If you don't need me, I *could* take the day off. You know, tend to some gardening. Darn a sock."

"You forget," Ellie said sweetly, "that I still have a key to your house." She smiled like a cat about to push a glass off a counter. "It would be a *shame* if your key wound up in the hands of the beachcombers."

Michael gasped. "You wouldn't dare."

"Wouldn't I?" Ellie let her words hang ominously in the air.

"I *do* have a new apron that I really wanted to wear tomorrow…" said Michael in a voice of surrender.

"He's on his way!" Alexis squeaked, turning her phone to show a small car scooting across a map. "Oh my gosh, my hair," she gasped.

She bolted upright and hurried to the restroom like the building was on fire.

"Her hair," said Michael, spearing another meatball with a toothpick. "If only life were that simple."

Olivia eyed Michael and took a sip from her beer. "Sorry to change the subject, but do you think you really have enough evidence to pin Victoria's murder on Noah based on hair? *Because*," she continued, before he could answer, "we really need to let Louie know."

"Detective Adams," said Michael. "I couldn't remember if I had told you that he is Olivia's uncle."

"Thanks," said Gerald. "I remember."

Michael turned back to Olivia and nodded slowly. "I think we have enough. His hair and his cologne put him at the scene of the crime. I wish we had—" He paused, snapped his fingers, and shoved his chair back from the table so abruptly Gerald flinched.

"Be right back," he called over his shoulder, speedwalking to the kitchen.

Gerald watched him go, then glanced at Olivia and Ellie and shrugged. "Must run in the family."

Chapter 47

Michael returned a minute later with a giant roll of deli paper tucked under one arm, a pair of scissors dangling from his finger, tape, and magic markers.

"He's finally lost it," said Olivia.

"Maybe he'll wrap himself," said Gerald. "World's largest bologna sandwich."

"The lack of imagination in this room is staggering," Michael announced, dropping the supplies onto an empty table. "I'm going to make a crime board. Gerald, give me a hand."

"It always starts like this," Gerald grumbled as he pushed to his feet. "They lure you in little by little."

"Hold this," Michael said, unrolling the paper. He measured out approximately six feet and, with Gerald's reluctant help, began taping the strips to the window. Ellie and Olivia joined in, helping to tape the edges.

A few minutes later, the group stepped back, admiring their handiwork.

"I have to admit," said Ellie, hands on hips, "it's a good idea."

For once in his life, Michael knew when to stay quiet and take the compliment gracefully. "Alright," he said, grabbing a magic marker. "Let's start with our prime suspect—Noah." He wrote NOAH in bold letters and circled it.

"The circle helps," Gerald muttered dryly.

"Before we start listing evidence, what's his motive?" Olivia asked. "Why would Noah kill her?"

"Jealousy," Gerald said immediately.

"That's jealousy for five," Michael called out.

"Why jealousy?" Olivia asked.

"Both Noah and Peter had a thing for Victoria. So… jealousy," said Gerald, defending his answer.

Ellie looked shocked. "Peter? No way. He despised Victoria. She made his life miserable."

"That's what he wanted everyone to believe," Gerald said. "But, trust me, Victoria and Peter were romantically involved."

Ellie looked like she'd taken a gut punch. She liked Peter. There was no way he was with someone like Victoria.

Gerald softened his voice. "The night Victoria was killed, Peter and Noah got into a fight over her. Plenty of witnesses."

"They didn't look like they'd been fighting," said Alexis, joining the group. "I saw Peter the next morning. He looked as fresh as a kitten."

"Yeah, believe me, it wasn't a fist fight," said Gerald. "If *anything* there may have been a dramatic slap or two. No way Peter or Noah were going to mess up their manicures."

Michael added *Motive* to the board, then added *Jealousy* beside it.

"Blackmailing," said Gerald.

"Gerald's on a roll," said Michael.

"Who was blackmailing who?" asked Ellie.

"We're not sure if Victoria already put her plan into action," Michael said. "But we know she was secretly recording her dalliances with cast and crew—and planned to use them to blackmail them."

Ellie recoiled. "That's horrible. Why would she do that?"

"I asked the same thing," said Michael. "The short version? Victoria was so volatile and undependable, nobody wanted to work with her anymore."

"So if she gathered enough dirt on enough people—" Olivia said slowly.

"She'd be protected," Michael finished.

"It's all on her alarm clock," Gerald added.

"Her alarm clock?" Ellie echoed. "This is getting more and more bizarre by the minute."

"The alarm clock was on her bedside table, it has a hidden video camera in it," Michael explained.

"Gross," Alexis shuddered.

Olivia nodded emphatically. "That's exactly what I said."

"Any idea who's on there?" asked Olivia.

"According to Chavon—"

"Chavon!" Ellie hissed. "You're going to believe that snake?"

"I actually think she was telling the truth," Gerald jumped in.

Michael silently thanked him—Ellie was obviously still a bit raw from how Chavon had mistreated her.

"We caught her with over a hundred thousand dollars' worth of jewelry and perfume in her purse," Gerald added.

"Sheesh," whispered Ellie.

"And… to stop us from calling the police, she agreed to tell us everything that she knew about Victoria," said Michael.

"Plus I made it *clear*, that if she lied, I'd hand her over to the police," Gerald added.

Ellie let out a tight breath. "Alright. Who's on it?"

"Noah, Peter, and David…" said Michael. "There may be others."

"David?" Ellie's jaw dropped. "The *director* David?"

Michael nodded, feeling bad for Ellie.

"Who wasn't she sleeping with?" Olivia blurted.

Michael and Gerald looked at each other and raised their hands in unison.

"We need to find out who's on that alarm clock," said Olivia. "And, we need to turn it over to the police."

"That's the plan," said Michael. "But I want to make a backup first. We all know from past experience how slow Lana Cove forensics can be…"

"Doesn't the clock have a SIM card?" Alexis asked. "I mean, you could just copy that."

"Yeah, but I don't have a SIM card reader for my laptop. Do any of you?" Michael asked.

His question was answered with a chorus of nos and headshakes.

"Mind if I take a look at the alarm clock?" asked Alexis. "I want to see if it has a USB port or something."

"Sure," said Michael. "It's in my coat pocket." He pointed to his chair and turned his attention back to the group. "Any other motives?"

"No, I think that's plenty," muttered Ellie. She looked shattered, the news hitting her harder than she expected. She'd grown quite fond of Peter—and many of the crew members.

"Alright," Michael pushed on. "Let's list the evidence we have against Noah."

"He was the last person seen with her before she died," Gerald said.

Michael nodded, writing it down.

"You found his hair on her pillow," Gerald continued, "and his cologne, which, as we said, puts him at the crime scene."

Michael continued writing.

"And you overheard his phone call, where someone told him to destroy all the evidence," Gerald finished.

"That will be easy for the police to confirm," said Olivia. "They can check his call log and run the number he called when Michael was under his bed—who knows, they might even be in his contacts."

"Most likely," Gerald agreed. "It had to be someone on the cast or crew because they were in the mansion."

"And…" Michael added as he wrote. "I have pictures of the evidence before he destroyed it."

"What was the evidence?" Olivia asked.

"He had a bunch of herbal supplements in his fridge—umcka, ginseng and echinacea," Michael said. "All kinds of little glass bottles."

"Did he have kava?" Olivia asked.

"Not that I saw, I only had time to do a quick search," said Michael.

"We should add that Chavon told us that Noah *always* knew where Victoria was."

"Yeah, I remember," said Michael.

"She was pretty sure Noah put a tracker on her phone—or something."

"If there was a tracker," Michael said, "there would most likely be an app or a website that he visited to track her."

"Forensics will be able to find that on his phone," said Olivia.

Michael stepped back, marker in hand. "What do you think? Enough evidence against Noah to give to Louie?"

"Definitely." Olivia nodded.

Michael turned to Alexis. "Figure anything out?"

"Oh yeah." Alexis perked up, setting her phone down. "Sorry, I was texting Neil." She held up the alarm clock and slid open a hidden panel. "You just need a phone charger. I downloaded the user guide. It's really simple: plug it into your computer, open the DCIM folder—that's where all the images and video files are stored—and copy everything over to your computer."

Michael nodded. "Perfect." He turned to Olivia. "I know you want to get this to Louie as soon as possible. But… can you give me until noon tomorrow? I want time to copy the files and get the hair sample analyzed. That way I can give him everything at once."

"I'm good with that." Olivia nodded.

"Perfect. Thank you." Michael smiled.

"Now that logistics are settled," said Ellie, setting her empty beer on the table, "who's next?"

Chapter 48

"He's here!" Alexis shot to her feet, smoothed her hair, and hurried across the café to the side door. Neil pressed his gloves against the glass, his eyes darting back and forth as if he didn't see her. Alexis flung open the door in a fit of laughter.

"My lady," he said with an exaggerated bow, taking her hand and kissing it. Alexis's cheeks flamed bright red.

"Come on," said Alexis, guiding him to the table. "I think you know everyone?"

"We haven't met." Olivia stood and shook Neil's hand. "I'm Olivia. It's a pleasure to meet you."

"Pleasure to meet you too," Neil said with a bright smile.

"Aren't you going to kiss my hand?" Olivia asked dryly.

Neil's eyes widened. "I—uh…"

"I'm messing with you." Olivia grinned, completely unfazed.

"Well," Neil said, quickly recovering, "I feel obligated now." He bowed slightly, kissing her hand.

Alexis burst into laughter, though a tiny spark of jealousy flickered beneath it.

An alarm sounded in the kitchen.

"That would be the oven," said Ellie, hopping to her feet. "Round two is ready."

"I'll give you a hand," said Michael, following her.

"Gerald!" Neil exclaimed, turning with genuine delight. "I didn't expect to see you here." He clapped Gerald on the back affectionately. "World's best security guard."

"Thank you," Gerald muttered. His face reddened from the praise.

Neil shrugged his coat off, hung it over the back of his chair and slipped into the seat beside Alexis. His eyes drifted toward the paper taped to the window. Gerald and Michael had hastily covered the notes about Noah beneath an extra strip of deli paper. However, the words *Motive*, *Jealousy*, and *Blackmail* still peeked out.

"Hm. Let me guess," Neil said with a grin, "murder mystery club? True-crime podcast?"

Alexis's heart stopped—she really didn't want to lie. Thankfully, Ellie and Michael returned at that exact moment with another six-pack of Maple Run Amber. Ellie slid a large plate of warm cinnamon donuts on the table and

Michael placed a fresh plate of sausage-and-cheese balls next to it. He turned and grabbed a fresh cup of apple cider from the table next to them and handed it to Alexis.

Another series of loud beeps filled the air, and Ellie hurried back to the kitchen.

Gerald dove in immediately. "These sausage balls are to *die* for," he declared. "Do you think Ellie would mind sharing her recipe?"

"I don't think Ellie would mind—" Olivia began.

"What's that?" Ellie asked, returning with a pot of decaf coffee and a precarious stack of mugs looped through her fingers.

"Gerald wants your sausage ball recipe."

"Of course," said Ellie, setting the coffee pot down. "I'll email it to you."

"Thank you, Ellie." Gerald smiled, his jaw moving nonstop. "They're so good."

Neil cracked open his beer, and reached for a sausage ball. He nodded appreciatively as he chewed. "If it's not too much trouble… could I be included in that email?"

"Of course." Ellie laughed delightedly.

"How are things going back on set?" Michael asked. "Things starting to feel normal again?"

"I think so," said Neil. "Camilla is a sweetheart. *So* talented. We do have a ton of reshoots, though—which has put us way behind."

"Yeah," Michael said. "When you unexpectedly lose one of the leads, that's gotta be tough on everyone."

Neil paused mid-bite, "There's a bit of a conspiracy about that. Lots of stuff on Insta and YouTube—TMZ isn't helping."

"Oh, like what?" Michael asked, far too innocently.

Alexis shot him a *Dad, STOP* glare. "I'm sure Neil doesn't want to talk about work."

"It's fine," Neil said with a small wave. "The rumor is Camilla has been right here in Lana Cove for weeks—and that if Victoria hadn't died, David was going to fire her."

"I saw that," Olivia said. "TMZ posted some drone footage from her beach house, showing her supposedly reviewing a script."

"Yeah, everyone thinks that Mouse shot the footage," said Neil. He grabbed a donut and offered half to Alexis.

"Mouse?" Michael looked around. The others appeared equally confused.

"Blond kid, surfer haircut—looks like he's still in high school," Neil explained.

"Oh yeah." Michael nodded. "I saw him flying a drone at the sleigh shoot. He looks like a teenager."

"Right?" Neil nodded. "They think it was him."

"A bit of a rebellious spirit." Michael grinned. "I can appreciate that."

"So, Peter was in on the whole replacing-Victoria thing, then?" Olivia asked.

"Peter? No? Why would you think that?"

"He's in the video from Camilla's beach house—"

"Peter? I thought that was David," Neil said, frowning.

Michael was halfway to saying *Actually his Mustang…* when Alexis shot him a warning look. "Yeah, you're probably right," Michael backpedaled.

"It wouldn't make sense anyway," Neil continued. He leaned forward conspiratorially. "Peter thought he had everyone fooled, but we all knew he had a thing for Victoria. He'd never meet with Camilla behind her back. Peter's loyal, he wouldn't have betrayed her trust."

"I feel the same way," said Ellie.

Neil took a bite of his donut and eased back in his seat, a smile slowly growing. "I see what's going on." He glanced around the table. "Gerald's here. You've been discussing Victoria's death…" He crossed his arms and sucked at his teeth. "I believe I've stumbled into a full-blown investigation."

"I'm sorry, Neil," Alexis said earnestly. "It's kind of my dad's thing. He's helped the police solve a couple of murders and—"

"Please don't apologize." Neil's eyes sparkled with delight. "This is so cool."

"Are you sure?" Alexis let out an amused sigh of relief.

"Yes." He patted Alexis's hand reassuringly and turned to Michael. "So you've actually helped solve murders?"

"A few." Michael shrugged, trying and failing to look modest. "I don't like to brag, but I help out when I can."

"Dear Lord," Olivia muttered.

"Okay," said Neil, leaning in. "This is completely off the record, but I always felt the timing of Victoria's death was suspicious. Add to that, Camilla being prepped to step in…" He shook his head and held out his hands as if to say *what do you think?*

Michael matched Neil's lean, and then leaned in even further. Another inch and they'd be touching noses. "I was thinking about that," said Michael. "And I gotta tell you, something didn't sit right with me."

"Probably hemorrhoids at your age," Ellie muttered.

Olivia held back a laugh and tapped her beer bottle against Ellie's.

"If I were about to be canned," Michael continued loudly, ignoring Ellie's comment, "I would do *everything* I could do to fix things. Instead, it seemed Victoria went out of her way to create a hostile environment, and to tick off David."

"That's how some actors thrive," Neil explained. "They have to get worked up to perform—to get into character. But with Victoria… her personality ended up consuming everything and everyone around her."

Michael leaned back, and took a sip of his beer.

"If anything," Neil added, "Peter tried to help her. He tried to convince her that she was needlessly damaging her career."

"Who would you say had the most to gain from Victoria's murder?" Olivia asked.

"That's a good question," said Neil, rubbing his chin. "It's a bit convoluted, but here's what happened. The studio made a quick ten million off of her death."

"How?" asked Alexis.

"Studios insure their leads," Neil explained. "Since Victoria was most likely going to be fired, the studio made money… but it's a two-way street—we have to do a lot of reshoots, and the studio had to renegotiate with Camilla."

"I think the whole crew and cast benefited," said Michael. "I'm not trying to speak ill of the dead, but from what we could see, she did cause a lot of chaos."

"It's true," said Neil. "She was a ticking timebomb."

"That's sad," Michael said, shaking his head. "I remember when she first started out, she was nine years old."

"With the remake of *The Cat from Outer Space*." Neil smiled.

"A classic." Michael nodded. "Everyone said she was going to be the next Marilyn. It's a shame her legacy had to end like this." He sighed.

"Well this has been lovely," Alexis announced abruptly. She scooted her chair back and rose to her feet. "Neil, how would you like to take a little stroll through Lana Cove? The town has decorated Beach Street for Christmas. It's beautiful."

Neil blinked, pleasantly surprised. "Of course, my lady. I'll have Edmund bring forth the horse and carriage. We shall leave straightaway!"

"Thank you, my lord." Alexis curtsied. "We'll be back in a bit." She shot Michael an I'm-not-happy-with-you look.

Ellie waited until they were out of earshot before turning to Michael. "You," she said flatly, "are in *so* much trouble."

Michael looked from Ellie to Gerald.

Gerald simply nodded, and popped the last sausage ball in his mouth. "Yep."

Chapter 49

The night was over. Neil thanked Michael for the ride, gave Alexis a hug, and then climbed out of the car. He searched his coat for a moment, digging in his pocket for the remote.

"He should have waited in the car," said Michael. He was about to roll down the window when Neil triumphantly thrust his hand into the air.

Neil turned into the headlights, smiled, waved goodnight once again, and slipped through a narrow doorway beside the wrought-iron gate.

"Everything okay?" Michael asked tentatively, glancing over at Alexis, who looked miles away. "Did you have fun?"

She shifted in her seat, staring out the car window. "He said that I was like the little sister he never had." Her voice sounded as fragile as glass.

"I see," Michael replied softly. He looked skyward, silently asking the universe for guidance. Times like this, he always said too much, or too little. The universe seemed to whisper one word: *Listen.*

Alexis wrapped her arms around herself and rested her forehead against the cold glass. "It was so embarrassing, Dad. Like—who am I to think that someone like Neil Phillips, Hollywood movie star, would be interested in me?"

Michael felt a rush of words swell up inside him—he desperately wanted her to know how amazing she was, how anyone would be lucky to have her as a friend… or more. But Alexis was no longer a child. A part of being a dad was wanting to fix everything… to make everything okay… but the bigger part was knowing when not to.

"He's leaving in a couple of weeks," Alexis continued. "Off to New York. Then L.A." A single tear slowly slipped down her cheek. "He promised he would keep in touch… but I'm not stupid."

Michael nodded gently, letting her know he was there—fully present, listening.

Alexis turned on the radio, tapped impatiently through a few stations, then shut it off. Nothing felt right. Nothing would be right tonight. She shifted closer, resting her head on Michael's shoulder. Within moments, her breathing softened as she drifted into sleep.

"Thank you, universe," Michael whispered.

Chapter 50

Michael awoke with a start, his alarm clock proudly displaying five a.m. He lay still for a moment, staring at the ceiling, collecting his thoughts. He could hear water running from the opposite end of the house—Alexis was already awake. How she could function on just five to six hours of sleep—he'd never know.

He swung his legs over the side of the bed, admired his calves in the morning light, and then yawned loudly. He slid his bare feet into a set of elf slippers Ellie had given him last Christmas. Across the room, his laptop and Victoria's alarm clock sat atop his chest of drawers, silently mocking him.

Initially, he'd thought that he would be able to connect the alarm clock to his computer and download the files. Easy. But no—Alexis had "forgotten" to tell him that the footage was encrypted behind a three-digit passcode. After everything Alexis had been through last night, he didn't have the heart to ask her for help.

Hopefully she would be in better spirits this morning. And hopefully she knew some computer wizardry that could crack the code.

Michael shuffled toward the bathroom, the bells on his slippers jingling with each step. He flicked on the lights, hissing like a vampire. This was going to be a long day. After brushing his teeth, showering, and getting dressed, Michael padded through the house. He found Alexis stretched out on the sofa, already absorbed in her phone.

"Morning," she said, smiling up at Michael. "You ready to go?"

"Is that a trick question?" He smiled sleepily—relieved that she looked more like herself today. A bit of rest certainly helped.

"You're not going to believe this." She spun her phone toward him. "But I have *five* thousand new followers on Instagram. I'm practically an influencer."

"I can't even comprehend that," Michael said, shaking his head. "My author page has twenty-seven followers. And I'm pretty sure most of them are bots."

"Neil posted a photo and tagged me," said Alexis.

"So, now you're it?" Michael teased.

Alexis blinked at him, confused.

"Tagged. Never mind." He sighed. "It was a bad joke."

"Remember what you told me?" Alexis slid off the couch and grabbed her coat. "If you have to explain a joke—"

"It isn't funny," Michael finished with a nod.

"You don't post jokes like that on Instagram, do you?"

"I'm on Facebook," said Michael, a little wounded. "And no, I mostly post about what I'm writing."

"I'll have to take a look later," she said, pulling a knit hat over her hair. "Seeing that I'm an *internet phenomenon* now." She grinned. "Maybe I can give you some pointers."

"That would be great," Michael said warmly. She followed him through the kitchen, into the utility room, and into the garage.

"Do you think you could help me get into the alarm clock this morning?"

"I told you—you just need to plug in the charger."

"No, I tried. It's asking for a three-digit password."

"Three digits?" Alexis scoffed, climbing into the passenger seat. "That's what, a thousand possible combinations? Piece of cake."

"Yeah." Michael nodded, starting the car. "Maybe for you. But for me, it would take forever."

"Your generation makes me so sad," said Alexis, sighing dramatically.

"What's that supposed—"

Alexis lifted a single finger. "Quiet, please. Genius researching."

Michael smiled, easing his Miata out of the driveway.

"We can use Hashcat," said Alexis, fastening her seatbelt. "It's a brute-force program. It can crack a three-digit passcode in, like, fifteen minutes."

"How much is that going to set me back?" Michael asked, pulling out onto Ocean Crest Lane.

"A couple hundred dollars."

"A couple hundred dollars," Michael sputtered. "For three digits? Is it going to do the dishes? Fold my laundry? Perhaps teach me the language of love?"

Alexis snorted. "The software is free. My *expertise* is two hundred dollars."

"Great." Michael laughed. "Put it on my tab."

Chapter 51

Outside the towering Dagmeyer windows, a lazy parade of snowflakes danced and swirled in the wind. In the distance, Gerald's golf cart sat parked alongside Victoria's trailer. Today he was working with a studio representative to oversee the packing and shipment of all Victoria's belongings to her family in L.A.

Inside the mansion, the usual suspects lined up at the craft service table, piling their plates with delectable goodies and placing a myriad of coffee and hot beverage orders.

Across the room, Camilla, Ian, Neil, and Dillan huddled with David and Peter. According to Neil, they were rehearsing a bookstore scene first—and then shooting the sleigh sequence later that evening.

Michael had already sent Abraham the evidence *and* breakfast via Uber Connect, and was anxiously awaiting a reply. As soon as the morning rush slowed, he planned to grab Alexis and have her start cracking the alarm clock code.

Peter broke away from the group and made his way toward the craft service table. Alexis hurried forward to help him.

"Well," he said, doing a dramatic spin like a runway model, "have I finally stumped you?"

Alexis expertly dissected Peter's outfit. A vintage charcoal button-up sweater, a coral-colored shirt, and a beautiful tie consisting of a swirl of intricate blues, grays, and greens. A Movado watch peeked from beneath his sleeve.

"You look like you just stepped off a Paris runway," Alexis teased. "Should I start with the Armani glasses?"

"Too easy." He waved her guess aside and tapped the fabric pattern of his tie.

Alexis leaned toward him, taking in every detail. "That's a tough one." She closed her eyes, deep in thought. "I'm going to have to go with… Ferragamo?" she guessed.

Peter's mouth fell open. "That's *un-real*," he said, clapping his hands together.

"Thank you." Alexis blushed. "I *love* fashion."

"I thought for *sure* I had you this time." He shook his head. "I'm going to have to tell Alisha in wardrobe to step up her game."

"You do that," Alexis teased. "Did you want your usual Al Cappuccino?"

"I'm going to try something different today," he said, arching an eyebrow. "What was Camilla's drink? I can't remember the name."

"Oh, the Snowfall Latte."

"Yes. Yes. I'll have one of those, please."

Alexis gave a sharp nod and darted off. Peter checked his phone and moved down the table to where Ellie was finishing up with a couple crew members.

"Good morning, Ellie." Peter flashed a polite smile.

"Morning, Peter," she replied.

"Just a reminder—we're planning dinner at seven. But if you could have it ready by six-thirty in case we wrap early…" He lifted his eyes skyward, as if appealing to the wrap gods. "That would be amazing."

"Yes, sir," Ellie said. "We'll be ready."

"I know you will. You always are." Peter gave a gracious nod. "I've got all of these little boxes in my head—I like to make sure they're all ticked."

"I'm the same way," Ellie agreed. "Always better to be over-prepared—"

"—than underprepared," he finished for her.

"Here you go, Peter," Alexis chimed in, sliding his latte toward him.

He scooped up the latte and took a sip. "Camilla certainly has good taste."

"Or," Alexis smiled, "I have some serious skills."

"Ah ha." Peter laughed. "I think a little of both." He scooped up the latte and pointed playfully at her. "I'm going to strategize with Alisha. We'll get you next time. I promise."

"I'm counting on it." Alexis grinned.

Ellie gave Alexis a sideways look. "What's that all about?"

"Oh—we have a little game. I guess the designer for whatever he's wearing; he tries to stump me."

"Oh." Ellie gave her an amused smile. "I didn't know you were a fashion major."

"I'm a hybrid—fashion and economics." Alexis tossed her hair proudly.

Ellie glanced down at her own outfit. "Okay, how's mine?"

Alexis gave a tight smile. "It's… nice. I mean, it's a uniform, right?"

Ellie sighed, somewhat deflated. "I think your dad's trying to get your attention."

Out of view, beneath the table, Alexis connected the alarm clock to Michael's laptop and opened the Hashcat program. The computer emitted a soft tone, prompting her for the three-digit password.

"Try 1-2-3," Michael suggested, kneeling beside her. "Works for my voicemail."

Alexis stared at him, horrified. "You are *exactly* why cybercrime exists."

"I'm just kidding," Michael said quickly. "It's 3-2-1."

Alexis sighed, opened a folder, and launched an executable file. A dark window filled the screen. Rows of numbers began streaming downward. A progress bar appeared at the bottom.

Michael leaned in, watching the counter tick through combinations—001, 002, 003—far faster than the human eye could follow.

"You don't have to watch it," Alexis teased. "You know what they say, 'a watched brute-force decrypter never—'"

The scrolling stopped. A new line appeared. Passcode found: 7-4-1.

"—decrypts," she whispered.

"Is it done?" Michael whispered.

Alexis flashed him a triumphant grin. "Yep. And that's why you always have a teenager on standby when it comes to a murder investigation."

"Next time someone dies, you'll be the first person I call," said Michael.

"Thanks, Dad." Alexis closed Hashcat, unplugged the connection cable, and then reconnected it to the alarm clock. The laptop chimed as a window popped up, prompting for the passcode.

Alexis typed 741. The window vanished and was replaced by a simple menu.

PLAYBACK | FILES | SETTINGS

Alexis clicked FILES. A folder named DCIM opened, revealing hundreds of video files.

"Geez," Alexis whispered. "There's over two terabytes of data."

"I'm hearing dinosaurs," Michael said. "Or the title of my new book—*Terror Bites*—which technically could also be about dinosaurs. Missed opportunity for Michael Crichton."

"Please tell me you're kidding," Alexis groaned.

"I'm kidding, I know what a terabyte is," Michael assured her. "I just don't know what that means… timewise?"

Alexis shrugged, cocking her head to the side. "Transferring over a USB connection, probably thirty minutes or so—give or take."

"I can live with that."

Alexis created a folder on his laptop, selected the video files, and dragged them over.

"And now," said Alexis, standing with a small stretch, "we wait."

Chapter 52

Michael sauntered to the end of the table, watching Ellie wield a knife like a samurai, turning a tomato into a pile of tiny cubes in a matter of seconds. "Remind me to never make you angry."

"I bet you say that to all the ladies." She glanced up at his new apron. *Master baker at work—donut disturb.* "Finally, an apron I approve of."

"I want to show my range," said Michael. "I'm no one-trick-pony. I'm nuanced."

"Something's buzzing beneath your apron," Ellie pointed out. "Hopefully not your one-trick-pony."

"Hah." Michael smiled. He slipped his phone from his pocket. "It's Abraham." He ducked below the table, out of sight, to take the call.

"Hey, Michael, I've got the results."

"Are they a match?" Michael asked quietly.

"Yep, dead on. The medulla pattern and pigment distribution are identical."

"I'll trust your word on that." Michael chuckled.

"I emailed you side-by-sides, magnified two thousand times."

"Thank you so much, Abraham. I owe you *big* time."

"You're welcome. Catch up with you later."

"Sounds good. Talk soon."

Michael ended the call, opened the email, and tapped the photos. Even without being a forensic expert, the match was unmistakable. They were Noah's hairs. They could officially put him at the scene of the crime. It was time to talk to Detective Adams.

Ellie caught his eye as he stood. "What's the news?"

"The hairs are an exact match," said Michael. "As soon as the files finish transferring from the clock, I should take everything to Louie."

"I agree," said Ellie. She gave the setup a practiced once-over. "Alexis and I can handle things here."

"Are you sure?" Michael asked. "Remember our conversation? Glue?" He tapped his chest. "The person who holds this whole operation together."

"I remember." Ellie nodded. She removed a tomato and cleaved it in half with one slice of the knife. She turned, and gave a menacing look. "I remember."

Chapter 53

Detective Louie Adams stared at his screen, his face expressionless. The only sounds in the cramped office were the squeaking of his ancient chair and the soft *tap-tap-tap* of his fingers on the keyboard.

Even though Louie's chair looked like it had been acquired at a rummage sale, it was much nicer than the aesthetically deprived chair Michael sat in—worn-out leather, stretched thin over a wedge of board, the cushion so overused it was the perfect mold of someone else's buttocks. Probably several someones.

Michael let his eyes roam around the office. A clock hung behind Louie, its once-white face now yellowed with age. The second hand had given up entirely and hung listlessly, no longer wanting any part of the fascinating construct of *time*.

Certificates from Lana Cove Town events dotted his wall in a nonsensical pattern. Bored, Michael began reading them.

Turkey Shoot—*what is a turkey shoot?* he wondered. *Do they shoot actual turkeys? If so, that is incredibly barbaric.*

The next read: Turkey Run. *Do they chase them first and then shoot them? If so, his certificates were out of order. He'd inquire later.* There was nothing like this in Boston.

Between the certificates were two short shelves containing a jumble of books, dusty bowling trophies, and framed photos. Michael smiled at a picture of a much younger Olivia— braces, braided hair, severe bangs, standing beside a bicycle with pink tassels hanging from the handlebars. Another showed her in a softball uniform, crouched and ready to swing. A recent one sat on the desk beside Louie's mug. On the floor, against a dead plant, leaned a dry-erase board that read: *263 days since our last homicide.*

Michael was still puzzling over the milestone when Louie's voice snapped him back.

"And this Noah Cruise guy," Louie said suddenly, "he was the last one to see Victoria alive?"

Michael straightened. "Yes. I believe so. Unless you know something I don't know."

Louie crossed his arms, his lips sagged into a frown. "Why don't you tell me what you know."

"I know that on the night Victoria died, she was out with Peter Star at the Love and Groove Bar. Noah showed up some time during their date, and the two men got into a fight."

Louie perked up.

"I use 'fight' loosely… From what I was told, it was more like a slap fight. Noah emerged as the 'victor' and left with 'Victoria.'" Michael smiled. "See what I did there?"

"Who told you?"

"About the fight?"

"Yes, about the fight." Louie's gaze drifted toward the ceiling.

"Chavon, Victoria's assistant. She said part of her job was cleaning up Victoria's messes."

"I see." Louie nodded. "And where did Peter go from there?"

"Back to the mansion," said Michael. "Several people saw him there."

"Peter at the mansion," repeated Louie, scribbling on his notepad. "Perfect, and what about Noah and Victoria?"

"They went to Oliver's."

"Oliver's." Louie scrunched up his face, doubt written all over it. "That place is a dive."

"It's also where an A-lister can go and be left alone," said Michael.

"Hm." Louie nodded again. "Could be."

Louie tapped his pen on his pad, doodled something, and turned his attention back to

Michael. "How did Noah know where to find Peter and Victoria?"

"I was wondering the same thing," said Michael. "There are a couple of theories."

"Enlighten me," said Louie.

"Victoria loved attention and chaos. One theory is she texted Noah to make him jealous, and told him where she was. The second theory—given by Chavon—is Noah was tracking her. She said he *always* knew where Victoria was."

"Would make sense, and easy to do." Detective Adams scribbled a few notes in his yellow legal pad. "How did you know they went to Oliver's? Did Chavon tell you?"

"We found a receipt in the trash can in her trailer from Oliver's, timestamped 12:37, the night she died."

"So, you think that Victoria and Noah left Oliver's, went to her trailer—"

"I know they did. I found Noah's hair on her pillow," Michael interrupted. "You got the analysis sent to you from the lab."

"Yeah, I was going to ask you about that." Louie leaned over his desk, impaling Michael with his stare. "You snuck into Noah's room to obtain the sample *without* his permission?"

"There was no sneaking involved," Michael declared. "I knocked on his door, there was no answer—and that's when I heard it—a woman screaming bloody murder."

Louie rubbed his temples. "You heard a woman screaming?"

"Bloody murder—it turned out to be the television," Michael admitted. "But the actress was *very* convincing. And just to be safe, I searched the room. But in the end, it was a—"

"It was the television," Louie said, cutting him off. "And the pictures you sent me of the herbal bottles—they were in Noah's refrigerator?"

"Yes." Michael nodded.

"And *why* did you take pictures of the herbal bottles?"

Michael frowned. "I… don't understand the question."

Louie angled his head, giving Michael a long, pointed stare. "Highly concentrated levels of kava were found in Victoria's body."

"Okay…?" Michael shrugged, still not following.

"You must have known about the kava somehow," Louie pressed. "Otherwise, why photograph the herbs? You thought Noah used them to sedate Victoria."

"Of course I knew about the kava!" Michael exclaimed. "Why are we making such a big deal out of this? It was on the news, TMZ, practically everywhere."

"I'm just wondering," said Detective Adams, "because we received an anonymous tip about the kava from a Little Snuggles Pet Care."

"I hear they do great work," said Michael.

"There's an image from their CCTV," Louie began, rotating his monitor.

"Fine," said Michael. "I called in the tip from their phone. I ran out of minutes on my burner."

Louie dropped his pen onto his desk, clasped his hands, and leaned forward.

"You just reminded me that I owe them an apology," said Michael. "I told them I'd dropped off my cat, Whiskers—and while they searched for him, I used their phone."

Michael shifted in his uncomfortable chair, Louie stared at him, silently.

"I feel terrible." Michael scratched his forehead, unable to stop talking. "I pretended to be irate because they couldn't find Whiskers."

"Because Whiskers never existed."

"Yes. And then I yelled at Brenda. I was *so* in character. I told her that this wasn't the last she was going to hear from me—and I waggled a finger while I said it." Michael turned his gaze to the tile floor, which he noticed was in a desperate state. "Not my finest moment… but, that being said, I did order a fruit basket for her and a mylar balloon as an apology."

"You are a piece of work." Louie shook his head. "Why didn't you just tell me about the kava."

"Because it was the assumption of the police that this was not a homicide. Plus, with all due respect, the forensics would have missed the kava. Abraham told me that it metabolizes quickly, and if you're not looking for it, you're not going to find it."

Louie leaned back in his chair, studying him. "How did you figure out it was kava?"

"I can't take all the credit for that."

"Of course not." Louie sighed.

"Gerald thought that Taylor Smith—the other security guard—had his tea tampered with. He said he would never have fallen asleep on the job. Plus, Taylor's thermos went missing."

Louie picked up his pen and motioned for Michael to continue.

"Gerald found a paper cup in the golf cart. He said Taylor always poured his tea into a cup when he went on rounds. So, I sent the cup to Abraham. He found highly concentrated kava residue. We figured if the killer used it to sedate Taylor, chances were that he used it on Victoria as well."

Louie nodded slowly, jotting more details into his notebook. His expression softened—barely.

"I'm sorry," Michael continued. "*Everyone* insisted it was an accident. I thought the kava lead might nudge the investigation into a different direction."

Louie flipped to a new page. "So… you're not liking this Peter guy for the murder? You think it was Noah?"

"Peter was sleeping with Victoria—he seemed to really care about her. Plus, he returned to the mansion early. Noah was the last one with her." Michael lowered his voice. "Personal note—at this point, I think *everyone* was sleeping with Victoria."

Louie arched an eyebrow.

"Present company excluded," Michael added quickly. "The only thing that is problematic for me is the fact that he was prepping Camilla for Victoria's role behind her back, one week before her death."

"Camilla is the actress who took over Victoria's role?"

"Yes." Michael nodded. "Why would he do that if he loved her? It's almost as if he knew something was going to happen."

Louie leaned in. "You have proof of that?"

"That he was meeting with her?"

Louie seemed to have perked back up.

"Yep, one second." Michael unlocked his phone and scrolled through his gallery. "Here."

He crossed the room to Louie's desk and handed him his phone.

"What am I looking at?"

"The first image is drone footage of Peter and Camilla at her beach house. She's holding a script."

"How do you know that's Peter?"

"Swipe to the next photo. The black Mustang? That's his," Michael explained. "I did a little sleuthing—found out he rented it a couple weeks ago."

Louie's jaw tightened. "So he was *actively* involved in replacing Victoria—while sleeping with her?"

"I'm afraid so," said Michael.

Louie studied the photos a moment longer. "I've seen that black Mustang before."

"You have?"

"Yep." Louie popped a thumb drive into his computer and clicked a file labeled *CCTV_Beach_Access*. He then clicked on *beachaccess1221.mp4*, and the video popped to life.

Michael recognized the location immediately—the tiny access street that led to the beach near Victoria's trailer. The timestamp was 2:15 a.m., the night of her murder. A black Mustang, headlights off, rolled to a stop.

A figure stepped out—heavy black coat, baseball cap, hood pulled low. A gust of wind caught the hood, flipping it back. The mysterious figure froze, then yanked the hood back into place. He reached into his car and retrieved a black satchel. He closed the car door, looked around, then headed onto the sand and disappeared into the darkness.

Michael's stomach twisted. "If Noah was with Victoria until sometime after one, and *he* killed her… then according to the timing of this video, Peter would have arrived to find her dead. And… if he wasn't involved, he would have called the police."

"Yep," Louie agreed. "You see, I think Noah went back to the mansion and Peter showed up afterward and finished the job. I think the last piece of the puzzle is on that alarm clock."

"I'll get it." Michael hurried back to his chair, pulled a white paper bag from his coat pocket, and handed it to Louie.

Louie turned it over in his hands. "Have you viewed any of them yet?"

"Of course not," Michael said, the guilt creeping in. "Okay—okay, I *tried*, but it's encrypted. It needs a three-digit passcode."

Louie rolled his eyes and pushed back from his desk. "I'll get forensics on it. You stay right there. Don't touch *anything*."

Michael held up both hands. "I won't move."

The door clicked shut behind Louie, leaving Michael alone in the cramped office—just him, sitting in the world's most uncomfortable chair, and a very tempting police computer humming seductively on the desk, just a few feet away.

Chapter 54

The temptation was too much.

Michael did a quick sweep of Louie's office for cameras. Perfect.

He darted across the room and dropped into the detective's chair. He quickly pulled up the browser, opened Louie's email, hit *Compose*, and typed in his email address.

He waited a beat, listening. A shadow darkened the door and then continued.

Michael navigated to the folder marked *CCTV_Beach_Access*, dragged the video file into the email, and clicked *Send*.

More voices in the hallway. He could feel sweat trickling from his armpits down his side, his heart racing. He launched into clean-up mode. Navigating to the *Sent* folder, he deleted the email. Then he navigated to the *Trash* folder and permanently deleted any trace of the email he'd sent.

He closed the browser and raced back to his chair. The door handle turned just as he slapped his phone to his ear.

"Yes—yes, we're almost finished. I got it, artisanal bread," he said brightly.

Louie stepped into the office.

"I've gotta go," Michael said into the phone. "Louie's back."

He slipped his phone into his pocket, trying to ignore the fact that his left eye was twitching like a faulty neon sign. "Sorry, that was Ellie—they really need me back at the mansion."

Louie plopped into his chair, giving Michael a long, thorough look. He was either suspicious or in love. Neither were good options.

"Uhm," Michael shifted uncomfortably. "Anything else you needed?"

Louie's eyes drifted to his mouse… then up to the monitor… then back to Michael.

A long, tight pause stretched between them.

"No," Louie said finally. "I'm going to bring Noah and Peter in for questioning. If you see them, *not* a word."

"Of course." Michael nodded solemnly. "Not to anyone. Especially not Ellie or Alexis—they both have a soft spot for Peter."

Louie sighed heavily at Ellie's name, rubbing his forehead. "All I can say right now is… things aren't looking good for Peter."

Chapter 55

Michael had mixed feelings as he drove back to the mansion. He should feel elated about the investigation—like he'd cracked the case wide open. Instead, a heavy mix of sadness, dread, and second-guessing filled his mind.

He turned on the radio, hoping to lift his spirits. Paul McCartney was belting out a tune about a wonderful Christmastime. Michael glanced up at the rearview mirror—he felt like the Grinch. He was about to shut down a Hollywood Christmas production, of all things. Cast, crew, Ellie, Olivia, and Gerald would all lose their jobs—right at Christmas.

A life had been taken, Michael reasoned with himself. There was a murderer, and who's to say they wouldn't strike again? Especially if they felt like they may be exposed.

Alexis is going to be furious with me.

Michael pulled onto the side of the road, letting the car idle. He flicked on his hazards and took a deep breath.

Ellie and Olivia are going to lose their huge contract.

Thoughts kept pouring into his mind. It was unfair. He didn't need a Dickens story to tell him the future, he already knew. He pulled out his phone and tapped out a message to Ellie. Moments later, three unmarked black SUVs whizzed by—blue lights flashing. In a matter of minutes, everything would change.

He forced himself back onto the road—he needed to be there for Alexis. Just as the mansion came into view, Ellie's name appeared on the dashboard display. He clicked *Accept*, swallowing hard.

"Where are you?" Ellie's voice was tight.

"Pulling up to the gate now," said Michael.

"Louie's here," Ellie whispered sharply. "With half a dozen officers. They've taken Noah and Peter—David's about to lose it."

"They had some video of Peter…" Michael's throat tightened. "I'm at the gate. I'll be right there."

"Okay," said Ellie, breathless, ending the call.

Liam, the front gate security guard, looked up from his phone. Recognizing Michael, he waved him in. Michael continued down the drive, navigating around a riot of police cars—blue lights flashing—and parked beside the security shed. He hurried to the door and knocked—no answer.

"Great." Arms outstretched for balance, he jogged across the icy lot. A lone police officer stood by the entrance to the mansion, his face stern, unmoving like chiseled granite. Michael flashed his ID badge, dropped Detective Adams's name, and the officer stepped aside.

Michael entered, bracing himself. The air inside felt electric, buzzing with tension and fear—at odds with the festive holiday music chorusing through the air. The crowd converged on two officers as they attempted to establish some semblance of order. Everything was unraveling—and he was walking straight into the center of it.

Louie and Gerald broke from the chaos, flanked by a plain-clothed woman and man— Michael didn't recognize them. Detective Adams's team, no doubt. Gerald led them across the room and through the towering doors that led into the mansion proper.

Michael had barely shrugged out of his coat when Ellie and Alexis rushed over to him.

"What's going on?" Ellie whispered urgently. "What did Louie say?"

"They're going to bring Noah and Peter in for questioning." Michael drew a slow breath. "They've got footage of Peter parking his Mustang at the end of the access road around two in the morning. The same night Victoria died."

"No." Alexis shook her head, tears welling up in her eyes. "Are they sure?"

"They're pretty sure." Michael pulled her into his arms.

Ellie covered her mouth with her hand, stunned.

"What do you mean *pretty sure*?" Alexis demanded.

"The video is dark and a bit pixelated," Michael explained. "You can see Peter get out of the car, pull up his hood, and walk toward the beach—"

"And you're sure it's him?"

"It certainly looks like him but—" Michael turned to Alexis. "I have the video, do you think you can work your magic on it?"

Alexis took a step back, wiping her eyes with the back of her hand. "Of course."

"What are you thinking?" asked Ellie.

"If I was about to kill someone, I wouldn't make my presence so obvious, and I'd certainly have scoped out the site earlier for cameras."

"Unless you wanted to be seen," said Ellie.

"Come on," Michael urged Alexis to the craft service table. "I emailed it to myself."

"What about the evidence they have against Noah?" asked Ellie, following.

"I'm not sure," said Michael. "They can prove he was with her the night of her death," he said quietly. "And the fact that he destroyed evidence… is a big deal."

"Do you think they'll close the shoot?"

Before Michael could answer, a commotion swept through the set. A group of police officers escorted Noah and Peter through the crowd. Noah's face was ghost-white, lips pressed tight, eyes darting. Peter—always the model of stoicism and grace—looked deflated. His jaw trembled, and when he caught Alexis's gaze, something like heartbreak and shame flickered through him.

The whole room fell into a hush as the two men were guided toward the exit.

Alexis's face contorted, tears flowed freely down her cheeks, more determined than ever to help her friend.

Chapter 56

Michael's phone dinged. He took in a deep breath, afraid to look. *Gerald.*

They found Victoria's phone in Peter's room. Hidden in the fireplace.

Michael's stomach dropped. He glanced up at Alexis, bent over his laptop, fingers flying over the keyboard. The news had gone from bad to worse.

Not good, Michael texted back. *Thanks for the update.*

"What is it?" asked Ellie, eyes filled with concern.

Michael swallowed. "They found Victoria's phone… hidden in Peter's fireplace," he whispered.

Ellie looked crushed. She glanced at Alexis and shook her head, turning her gaze back to Michael. "We can't tell her yet. We wait to hear from Louie, okay?"

"I agree." Michael nodded. "She's already been through enough."

Across the room, David's voice boomed through a speaker. "Everyone quiet. Everyone settle down."

The voices quieted from a rumble to a soft murmur. David surveyed the crowd, making direct eye contact with anyone still speaking.

"Could someone please"—he drew a finger across his throat—"with the Christmas music?"

Michael slipped his remote out of his pocket and tapped the *mute* button, silencing the music.

David looked around for a moment, surprised, and then continued. "As you are aware, Noah and Peter have been taken in for questioning. This is *typical* of any police investigation involving a death."

"Are we shutting down?" a nervous voice called out from the crowd.

"Absolutely not," said David, his voice ringing with confidence. "They will be questioned, as may others, but I'm confident they will be back shortly. That being said, I *insist* that we continue to stick to our schedule."

A rumble of voices filled the room.

"Quiet down, people," said Kyle Makita, the Assistant Director.

David waited a beat and began speaking again. "Neil, Camilla, Dillan, and Ian, continue rehearsing the bookstore scene."

The four actors nodded in unison.

"I fully expect Noah to be back tonight. However—" David looked out into the sea of people. "Andrew," he nodded to a thin, balding man with a ponytail, "you'll be in charge. If you have any questions about what you're supposed to be doing, check with your supervisor." He clapped his hands. "Back to work, everyone!"

"You heard the man," said Kyle. "Let's make this happen."

Slowly, order was restored on the set. People felt like they had a purpose, a job to do. Gerald emerged through the towering doors into the Dagmeyer Room, followed by two officers, evidence bags in tow.

He met Michael's eyes and gave a subtle headshake, then followed the officers out the door, into the cold.

Chapter 57

Michael mindlessly scooped a fruit mix into a large bowl and loaded an assortment of yogurt into a chiller. He and Ellie had been working nonstop for the past hour, feeding a nervous crew, when Kyle Makita—immaculate in a white cable-knit sweater and brown cords—strode up to the craft service table.

"We'll still need dinner tonight for the talent and crew," he said curtly, dispensing with all pleasantries.

"Of course," Ellie replied smoothly. "We've already begun prep. We'll be fully ready by six-thirty."

Kyle cast a suspicious glance at Alexis, still hunched over Michael's laptop. "I've noticed she's been at that for quite a while."

"Yes," Ellie said carefully.

"Hm. Curious."

"She's working on inventory—" Ellie began.

But Kyle was already moving down the table with the predatory intent of a shark, eyeing its prey. He stopped in front of Alexis, leaning into her space.

"Hello, Mr. Makita." Alexis smiled up at him.

"What's got you so busy?" He eyed her as one would a dessert platter.

"I'm replenishing our inventory for tomorrow morning," she said lightly. "We go through a *lot* of food, as I'm sure you're well aware."

"I see." Kyle gave a curt nod—then did the unthinkable. Without warning, he grabbed the laptop and flipped the screen toward himself.

Michael saw red. He took a step toward Kyle, but Ellie snagged him by his apron strings, reeling him back.

"No," she whispered. "She's got this."

A sudden look of disappointment washed over Kyle's face when he realized that Alexis was, in fact, entering data into an inventory system. He gave her a pitiful excuse of a smile, then stalked back toward Ellie.

"I'll take a latte, oat milk," he said curtly.

Ellie nodded, made the latte, and handed it to him with a tight smile.

Cup in hand, Kyle spun on his heel and marched toward the crew—clearly ready to make someone else's life miserable.

As soon as he was out of earshot, Ellie and Michael hurried over to Alexis.

"How did you fool him?" Michael blurted.

Alexis grinned in triumph. "I've been telling you—I've got mad skills."

"But, how on earth did you get into *my* inventory system—on your dad's laptop?" Ellie asked, genuinely baffled.

"I didn't," said Alexis. "While you two were distracting him, I Googled *Coffee Shop Inventory Database*, took a screenshot, saved it as my desktop wallpaper, and moved my mouse around like I was working. He fell for it."

"That's brilliant," said Ellie. "Frightening, but brilliant."

"What's brilliant?"

The trio looked up to see a worn-out Gerald standing in front of them.

"Alexis's computer skills," said Michael.

"Alright." Gerald nodded, guessing there was some subtext he was missing.

"I'll fill you in later," said Michael. "Got any news for us?"

Ellie noticed Kyle glancing over again. "Gerald—act like you're getting food. Kyle's been on the warpath for some reason." She discreetly motioned for him to follow her toward the far end of the table.

Gerald grabbed a plate and plucked up a bagel. "Can you cut this in half and toast it, please?"

"Absolutely." Michael made a big show of slicing the bagel.

Gerald lowered his voice. "They took Peter and Noah's laptops and phones."

Michael slid the two halves into the toaster and pressed the lever. "Would you like your bagel rare, medium rare, or well done?"

"Medium well," Gerald deadpanned, long past being surprised by Michael's quirks.

"The good thing," said Michael, "if they've done nothing wrong, the devices can help prove their innocence."

Ellie rejoined them and handed Gerald a steaming black coffee.

The toaster dinged and ejected the bagels. Michael snatched the two halves out of the toaster with two quick *ouch ouchs* and dropped them onto the plate.

"Here you go, sir—medium well."

Gerald grabbed a small tub of cream cheese and began slathering it on. "Remember the hat Peter was wearing? The one in the beach house video?"

"Yeah," Michael said, already bracing himself.

"They found that in Peter's room." Gerald frowned. "Under a sofa cushion."

"That makes no sense. Why would he hide it under a sofa cushion?"

"Kyle's heading over," Ellie warned under her breath.

"That's my cue," Gerald muttered. He gave a quick thanks and made for the door.

Kyle paused halfway across the floor, locking eyes with Ellie. *What was his problem?*

Then, without a word, he spun on his heel and headed toward David, who waved him off with the flick of a hand.

Ellie watched the man carefully. "Something is definitely off."

"Guys," Alexis whispered urgently, motioning them over. "You've got to see this."

Chapter 58

Michael slid into the van, punched *Start*, and shifted into reverse. He spun the wheel hard and gunned the gas.

Moments before, he'd fired off a cryptic text to Detective Adams: *On my way, urgent!*

Lana Cove's Police Station was about fifteen minutes from the mansion, but it felt like hours when Michael finally slalomed into the parking lot. He leapt from the van onto the icy asphalt, regretting it instantly as his feet flew out from under him, sending him careening into a cavernous cement drainage ditch filled with water and ice.

Michael lay still for a moment, staring at the sky, slowly moving his body until he was certain nothing was broken. And then, on hands and knees, he crawled out of the ditch. His rear end hurt, his palms were scraped, and the seat of his pants was ripped and wet, but that didn't stop him. He knelt and picked up his laptop— miraculously it was still in one piece.

He limped across the parking lot. Officer Morris stood at the entrance wearing a Santa hat and a ridiculously huge smile on his face, clapping. He pointed gleefully to the CCTV camera above the door. "I'm going to watch that on repeat. May even add a soundtrack."

"Remember who brings the donuts to the station every Christmas," Michael groaned as he sloshed by him.

"Look who suddenly can't take a joke." Officer Morris smirked.

"I need to talk to Louie right away. It's urgent."

"He's interrogating someone. And we *both* know what happens when he's interrupted." Officer Morris lifted his brows in warning.

But Michael was already moving, pushing past him and barreling down the hall. He pounded on the door labeled *Interview 1*.

The door flew open with a *bang!* An enraged Detective Adams stormed out, anger etched across his face. "What? What is it?" he barked, jabbing a finger into Michael's chest.

"You've got the wrong guy!" Michael yelled back—startling himself almost as much as Louie.

"What do you mean?" Louie grabbed Michael by the arm and hauled him down the hall to his office. He shoved him inside and slammed the door behind him.

"You've got five seconds to explain yourself," Louie growled, hands braced on his desk.

Michael's phone buzzed. He glanced at the screen. A text from Gerald read: *Found it!*

"Okay." Michael held up his laptop, like a peace offering. "May I?"

"By all means." Louie's voice was filled with anger.

Michael set the laptop on Louie's desk, opened a folder, and clicked on a video file named *CCT_RT_651B*. It was the exact same video Louie had shown him before, only this copy looked… different.

"How did you get this video?" Louie thundered. "Did you steal police property?"

"No." Michael looked shocked. "Gerald used to be a cop. He has friends at the public works office—they pulled the footage for him."

The answer seemed to appease Louie; his shoulders relaxed a smidge as he leaned in.

"Look," Michael said, forwarding the video until he reached the moment when the figure stepped out of the black Mustang. The man's hood blew back. Michael slowed the playback to quarter-speed. "Now watch."

Louie moved forward until he was inches from the screen.

"How come your video looks so much clearer?"

"Alexis cleaned it up for us. AI enhancement," Michael admitted. He tapped a key, and the hood whipped back in ultra slow motion. "Watch closely. You see that flash?"

Louie narrowed his eyes. "Yeah, I saw something. What am I looking at?"

"Alexis froze that frame and enhanced it," Michael said. "That flash—right there, it's a wedding ring."

Louie squinted. "Well, I'll be."

"And not just that." Michael tapped an arrow. "Watch what happens when he reaches up to pull his hood back on."

"He's wearing a bracelet," said Louie.

"Not just any bracelet." Michael zoomed in closer. "That's a David Yurman cable bracelet. Signature design."

"So… who is it?"

"That, my friend, is David Brooke. The director."

Louie nodded, all of the anger and rage dissipated as he stared at the computer.

"And… that's not all," Michael added. He pulled out his phone and turned the screen toward Louie. "Gerald found this. The missing security logbook—the one stolen from the guard station. It was hidden in David's room."

Louie snatched his coat from the back of his chair. "I'm still mad as the dickens at you—so don't think you're off the hook." He threw the door open and sprinted down the hallway, leaving Michael standing alone in the middle of his office, unsure whether to feel proud… or terrified.

Chapter 59

David's face drained of all color as Detective Adams and a phalanx of officers descended on the set. For a heartbeat, he stood frozen, but then quickly recovered, pointing a defiant finger at Louie, who was intruding on his domain.

"If you want to speak to me, you can make an appointment," David spat. "We're in the middle of a rehearsal, and this is *private property*."

"I've already spoken to Mr. Marlow," Louie replied calmly. "He's aware that you have been named a suspect in a murder investigation."

A ripple of horrified gasps spread through the cast and crew.

"I'm going to have your badge for this!" David yelled, his voice trembling with rage. "You can't make unfounded accusations like that!"

"Mr. Brooke," Louie said firmly, "we have video evidence *and* physical evidence. You can come with us the easy way—or…"

David hung his head, his shoulders sagging in defeat. "Fine." He removed his headphones, placing them on the monitor, his hands trembling so badly they nearly slid off.

He took two slow steps toward Detective Adams and then—with surprising agility—bolted across the set, hurdling over a couch and crashing through the towering doors, disappearing into the mansion.

The officers gave chase, Michael and Gerald close behind.

David bolted up the main staircase two at a time. He sprinted past the balcony and then slipped into a room at the far end of the hall, slamming the door behind him.

Louie reached the landing just as the officers fanned out, surrounding the door.

He pounded on the door with his fist. "David, please—just talk to us."

A sudden whoosh, followed by a heavy bang, came from inside the room.

"Sounds like he's going onto the balcony!" one of the officers exclaimed.

Louie took two steps back and drove his foot into the door, splintering the frame. The door crashed inward, slamming against the wall. On the balcony, David was clambering onto a chair.

"Wait—don't move!" he ordered, throwing out his arms to halt the officers.

David pulled himself onto the narrow wooden railing, covered in a thin layer of ice.

Below him, a sheer twenty-five-foot drop to cement and arched stonework.

The winter wind howled, ripping at his clothes, buffeting him violently.

"Don't come any closer!" David warned, his voice raw with emotion. His feet slipped, arms windmilling wildly as he fought to maintain his balance.

"David," Louie said gently, slowly moving toward him. "Don't do this. We can work this out. Just come down."

"No!" David barked bitterly. "My life is destroyed. She destroyed me."

"Think of your wife," Louie pleaded. "Your daughter. The people who love you."

"Stop!" David roared. "Please. Just. Stop." One foot slipped. He staggered sideways—caught himself.

He turned his head just enough for Louie to see the tears streaking down his cheeks. "Tell my wife—and little girl—that I love them."

"You tell them," Louie said, moving closer. "You tell them."

"I'm sorry."

David looked out at the ocean. "What I've done… is unforgivable." He closed his eyes, and slowly lifted his arms, opening them, as if surrendering himself to the wind.

"Goodbye—"

Wump!

Suddenly, David was hurled backward off the railing, breath exploding from his lungs as a drone struck him with a gut-wrenching thud to the chest. He toppled backward onto the balcony floor.

Louie lunged. He dropped to his knees and grabbed David by the shoulders, dragging him safely inside. David collapsed against him, sobbing uncontrollably.

Outside in the courtyard, a young man in a hoodie lowered a drone controller and walked away.

The Mouse had saved David's life.

Chapter 60

Louie stomped the snow off his boots and hurried into the café, chased by a gust of icy air. He leaned in to hug Olivia, brushing a cold kiss against her cheek.

"Ah!" Olivia shrieked, recoiling. "Go warm your lips up on some coffee!" She laughed, locking the door behind him.

"Louie," Ellie called, waving him over.

He waved back, and crossed the café, leaving a trail of wet size-ten footsteps behind him. "Evening, everyone," he said, circling the table to give Ellie a hug, and an affectionate pat on the back.

"Here—let me help you," Ellie said, helping Louie shrug out of his bulky police jacket.

Olivia reappeared and set a steaming cup of coffee in front of him before squeezing into a chair between Alexis and Michael.

"How are things going?" Olivia asked, a worried look on her face.

"Like a three-ring circus," Louie rasped. His voice was rough, his eyes tired. "Media is everywhere. Half of them camped outside the station." He took a sip of coffee and closed his eyes.

Ellie waited until he settled before asking. "So, David confessed to everything?"

Louie nodded heavily. "Yeah. He had to. Thanks to Victoria's clock, we had video of him engaged in—ah." His eyes fell on Alexis, his face turning bright red. "Let's just say he was doing things a married man shouldn't be doing."

Alexis's eyebrows shot up, amused at Louie's discomfort. Ellie cleared her throat loudly.

"Did he say why she was blackmailing him?" asked Olivia.

Louie sighed. "There's a *certain* franchise— which I'm not at liberty to reveal. Victoria was auditioning for the female lead. She wanted David to speak to the director—I guess they're best friends. David told her she was out of her mind… and that's when he received an email with the first video."

"Like Chavon said," Michael chimed in. Ellie rolled her eyes at the mention of Chavon's name.

"She threatened to send the video to his wife and to the press," Louie said. "That would have ended him."

"So he kills her… and sets up Peter and Noah to take the blame." Ellie shook her head.

"The downfall of one of Hollywood's biggest directors," Michael breathed.

"The whole situation is horrible," said Olivia. "It affected so many people's lives."

"I know it's an open investigation," said Michael, "but let me know if I'm pretty close."

Louie rubbed his face. "Let's see what you've got." He motioned for Michael to continue.

"David waits until Noah leaves Victoria's trailer. David shows up, gives her some kind of excuse, and they have a drink. He spikes hers. She passes out—and he poses her outside the door, and snaps off the key in the lock. According to Abraham, the kava mixed with alcohol slows the heart rate so much, she would have gone quickly."

"Yeah. That's about the gist of it." Louie nodded, clearly uncomfortable with the conversation.

"And Peter…" Alexis asked hesitantly, "he's innocent, right?"

"I was just about to ask the same question." Ellie smiled.

Louie nodded. "As far as we can tell, Peter had nothing to do with Victoria's death. David tried to frame him—planted Victoria's phone in his room, used Peter's laptop to look up kava interactions…"

"I knew it couldn't be Peter." Ellie sighed with relief. "Although… I am disappointed in his choices."

"What about the Mustang?" asked Olivia.

"David had Peter rent it for him. Peter actually never drove it," Louie explained. "Typical request for an AAD."

Gerald, who had been silent until now, leaned forward. "And Noah?"

"Noah." Louie snorted. "He's a piece of work."

"Not his biggest fan, then?" asked Michael.

"Not by far." Louie frowned. "He boasted about rubbing shoulders with the top directors and producers—convincing naïve crew members and aspiring actresses that he could open doors for them."

"Disgusting," said Ellie.

"The only door he could open was his bedroom." Michael frowned.

"I thought he was in love with Victoria," said Olivia. "Isn't that what Chavon said?"

"Yeah." Michael and Gerald nodded in unison.

"Well," sighed Louie, "it looks like he had a lot of love to give. The night Victoria was killed, he hooked up with a crew member named Crystal Voss… so he has an alibi."

"So it was her lipstick on the wineglass," said Michael.

"Yep." Louie nodded.

"What about the phone call—where he panicked?"

Louie nodded slowly. "He wasn't panicking about killing Victoria. Noah's big into herbs and health food. He thought that all of the herbs in his fridge made him look guilty."

"Chavon mentioned she thought Noah was tracking Victoria," said Gerald.

"She was right," said Louie. "I still need to speak with her. We confronted Noah—he claimed he was simply looking out for Victoria. He hid a tracker in the hem of her coat and her purse."

"That's super creepy," whispered Alexis. Ellie and Olivia nodded in agreement.

"What a mess," Ellie murmured. "I feel sorry for his wife and kids."

"Lesson learned," said Michael. "It's why I don't date gorgeous models and movie stars." He leaned back in his chair and crossed his arms. "Too much trouble."

"Yeah," snorted Olivia, "*that's* the reason."

"I have very discerning tastes." Michael sighed dramatically.

Louie set his coffee down. "I've got a question. What happens now? Is everyone out of a job?"

Michael shifted uncomfortably in his seat. He could have gone the entire night without that question.

"I can answer that," Alexis announced with unexpected enthusiasm. "I got a little insider information, but—" she gazed around the table suspiciously—"should I have you all sign an NDA or can you guys keep a secret?"

"Of course we can keep a secret," said Michael. "We're all family here… with that one weird uncle." He let his eyes drift toward Gerald.

"You're lucky Detective Adams is sitting right there," Gerald smirked.

"Don't let me stop you," said Louie, giving Gerald a conspiratorial wink.

"Do you want to hear the news or not?" Alexis huffed impatiently.

"Yes, *please*," said Ellie, shooting the men a warning look. "Ignore their buffoonery."

"They're going to close production for a week," said Alexis, unable to control her excitement. "And… then they're bringing in Robert Mangold to finish the movie!"

Ellie gasped. "Robert Mangold, the director of *When Lips Meet*?"

Michael looked at Gerald who replied with a don't-ask-me shrug.

"They said lipstick sales across the country went up two hundred percent!" Ellie continued.

"I loved his dog-park romantic comedies," Olivia laughed. *"Please Re-Leash Me, Let Me Go."*

"Oh, and the sequel, *Collard Again.*" Ellie laughed.

Michael, Louie, and Gerald traded confused looks. None of them had the faintest idea what they were talking about.

Louie glanced at his watch, finished off his coffee, and rose from the table with a weary stretch. "I've gotta get back to the station, finish a few things."

Olivia stood and wrapped Louie in a big hug. "See you tomorrow night at the Christmas party? No excuses this time about having to work late."

"I promise, I'll be there." He turned to Ellie and gave her a warm smile. "Ms. Ellie, thank you for everything. I'll see you tomorrow."

"Night, Louie." Ellie smiled warmly.

A chorus of goodnights followed him as he headed for the door. He gave one last wave, and stepped out into the snowy darkness.

"I guess I should be heading out as well," said Gerald, rising. "Thank you, Ellie. Olivia." He nodded to each of them.

"You're coming to the party too, right?" asked Olivia.

"I didn't know I was invited." Gerald blushed, genuinely surprised.

"Of course you are," Olivia declared. "You're an honorary member of our crazy little family."

"That is," Ellie gave a playful wink, "if you can put up with us on Christmas Eve."

It didn't seem possible, but Gerald's face grew even redder. "Thank you," he said gruffly. "I wouldn't miss it for the world."

Chapter 61

Night settled over Lana Cove. Snowflakes floated and danced on the invisible contrails of an icy breeze, glistening in the radiant glow of the streetlights. A row of cars filled Olivia's driveway and the street in front of her house. Her yard glittered and sparkled beneath the porch light, as if it were dusted in diamonds. Laughter and music spilled from beneath her door, filling the night.

Inside Olivia's house, the party was going at full swing. Her open floor plan connected the kitchen and dining room, divided only by a marble-topped island covered in holiday favorites: spiraled ham slices, a mountain of mini quiches, warm sausage-and-cheese balls, a bowl of sugared pecans, and a tray of Ellie's famous cinnamon-dusted donuts. A crystal punch bowl sat in the center, filled with sparkling cranberry cider.

The space opened directly into the living room, where vaulted ceilings rose like the inside of a cathedral. A two-story stone fireplace crackled with a toasty fire. Couches and armchairs were arranged in cozy clusters, so no matter where you sat, you felt like you were a part of the conversation. A stunning white upright piano dominated the back of the room.

Christmas music swirled and twirled with laughter and conversation. Kids excitedly darted between clusters of adults—their hands filled with sugar cookies and treats—while guests nibbled from small plates and napkins, sipping cider and wine. The scent of pine, cinnamon, roasted ham, and freshly baked rolls drifted warmly through the rooms.

"This is amazing," said Michael, giving Olivia a hug. "I may never leave—this is my third plate."

"Next time, try eating the food, it's much better," Olivia joked.

"Good one." Michael laughed. "If the café thing doesn't work out, maybe you could be a comedian… but seriously, you've outdone yourself."

"Thank you, your lovely daughter was a big help."

"Any praise you feel you need to bestow upon Alexis, you can heap them on me."

"Is that so?" Olivia gave him a coy smile.

"I'm responsible for *all* of my daughter's best qualities."

"Uh huh. I'll try to remember that." Olivia eyed Michael's Christmas sweater. A mix of green and red intersecting triangles—it was, in one word, *hideous*. "Knead Me At Your Own Risk," she read aloud.

"What do you think?" Michael asked. "I brought others."

"You brought other sweaters?" Olivia laughed. "Who are you? Madonna?"

"A performer always keeps his audience guessing." Michael said, crossing his arms.

"Dad, are you bothering Olivia again?" Alexis asked, joining them.

"Of course not—"

"Sure." Alexis grasped Olivia's hand and gave her a gentle tug. "Ellie needs our help corralling the children. Santa's going to be here in about five minutes."

"Here." Olivia handed Michael an empty plate with a crumpled napkin. "Now you can have fourths."

Remembering his assigned party duty, Michael sauntered into the kitchen and inspected the trash situation. He was just in time, the tower of trash was about to topple. He replaced the bag, washed his hands, and filled the dishwasher with mugs and plates that had collected on the countertop.

Across the room, he could see Alexis and Olivia chasing a sugar-fueled gaggle of children in a failed attempt to orient them toward the piano.

Oh, to be young again, Michael thought.

At last year's holiday party, Michael had played a little Christmas melody for everyone, and the guests had thoroughly enjoyed it. To his delight, Olivia asked him to play something for the kids while they waited for Santa. He jumped at the chance.

A smile crossed his face as a red-faced Alexis sprinted past him again. He closed his eyes, thankful for the chance at spending time with his daughter.

He grabbed a few mugs from the drying rack, sat them on the island, and wandered over to the fireplace where Gerald and Louie were talking.

Louie gave an exaggerated groan as he approached. "Here comes trouble."

"Careful standing so close to the fireplace… all that polyester," Michael teased.

"You've got a lot of room to talk with that sweater," grumbled Louie. "I should take you in for murdering fashion."

Gerald chuckled, and gestured to the party with his mug. "Olivia does a great party."

"I'll say," said Michael.

Gerald reached in his pocket and pulled out an unwrapped sucker, completely covered in gray lint, and handed it to Michael. "Merry Christmas," he deadpanned.

"Thanks, Gerald." Michael popped the sucker into his mouth without giving it a second glance, reveling in Gerald's shocked expression.

Louie raised his eyebrows, clearly amused. "I was telling Gerald that since Ramone retired, we could certainly use someone to take his place."

Michael gave Gerald a surprised look. "You're thinking about—"

"No, no, no," Gerald interrupted, waving his hands, his cocoa slopping precariously in his cup. "Not me. I was thinking about Taylor. Full-time job, benefits. Something secure."

"That's a great idea," said Michael. "Especially since he has a family to take care of."

"I'm meeting with him Thursday," said Louie. "We talked briefly on the phone—seems like a nice guy."

"He is," Gerald said immediately, leaving no room for doubt.

"Louie, you should talk to Abraham Leung about being a consultant," Michael added. "He could be a huge asset to your forensic team. He—"

"Sorry to barge in," said Ellie, giving the men a quick apologetic smile. She turned to Michael. "Santa's going to be here in about two minutes."

"Gentlemen." Michael nodded. "That's my cue."

He crossed the room to the piano where a semi-circle of children sat waiting. He circled the piano, turned, and bowed dramatically to the children, making them giggle.

"Tonight, I shall perform a Christmas concerto!" he announced with a booming voice. He bowed to the children again, and sat on the bench, facing away from the piano. He stretched out his arms and began to play.

The children laughed hysterically.

"You're facing the wrong way!" a child shouted from the group. She smacked her forehead and shook her head.

"Oh, yes." Michael acted surprised. "Someone must have moved my piano." He spun on the bench facing the piano. "There it is!" He held out his arms, rolled his wrists in circles and wiggled his fingers. "Do you guys want to help me sing a Christmas song?"

"Yes!" the children shouted, rocking from side to side with excited giggles.

"Alright." Michael nodded solemnly. "This is a famous song I used to sing to my daughter when she was young. Now, she's older than me!"

A chorus of groans and laughter swept through the kids.

Michael played several dramatic chords on the piano, and then, with great seriousness, began singing, "Twinkle, twinkle little star, how I wonder—"

The children looked at each another and burst out laughing.

"That's not a Christmas song!" a little boy shouted out through giggles.

"It's not?" Michael gasped in mock horror. "I'm sure it is."

"Noooo!" the children yelled.

"Oh, you're right—wrong sheet music." Michael flipped an imaginary page and gave the children a conspiratorial wink. "Alright then. Here we go!"

He launched into the opening lines of "Santa Claus Is Coming to Town." "You better watch out. You better not cry. You better not pout—"

Within seconds, the room transformed. Michael's heart swelled with joy as the children and parents began singing along—swaying back and forth, arm in arm.

And on the final chorus, right on cue, George Owens—Lana Cove's official Santa—joined in. George had played Santa ever since Ellie and Olivia were children. It took but a moment before the children spotted him. Instantly, George was surrounded by excited children, dancing and throwing their arms around him.

While all the party-goers were swept up in the magic of the moment, Alexis slipped Neil and Peter through the doorway. Neil, not wanting to cause a stir, had his hair-and-makeup assistant work a little Christmas miracle—changing his appearance slightly so he was unrecognizable. He hid behind a Santa hat, thick-framed black glasses and a shadow of stubble. At first glance, he looked like a visiting college kid, not a world-famous actor.

Alexis gave Neil a quick hug, then turned to Peter, who held out his hand. "Peter," she tsked, batting it aside and wrapping him up in a tight hug instead. "I'm so glad you came."

"Thank you, Alexis." He gave her a genuine, heartfelt smile. "I got you a little something."

He handed her a box, the size of a deck of cards, wrapped in silver paper, with a red ribbon.

"I'm going to grab some food." Neil winked, adjusting his glasses. "Meet you over there."

"Okay." Alexis smiled, watching him head for the food before turning her attention back to Peter. "Thank you—but I wasn't expecting anything. I'm just happy you're here."

"It's something small," he assured her. "See if you can guess."

"Oh I see, a challenge!" Alexis grinned. She carefully peeled away the silver wrapping, lifted the lid and froze. "Peter," she gasped. "This is—wow."

She touched the pendant lightly with her fingertip, her eyes bright with surprise.

"It's beautiful."

"I thought it suited you," he said simply, clearly pleased. "Well...?" he asked, a mischievous look filling his eyes.

Alexis lifted the necklace—a fine gold chain with a round mother-of-pearl pendant. A small diamond sparkled from the center, catching the light as it moved.

"Cartier," she declared confidently.

"Right you are." Peter grinned.

"Did you have any doubts?"

"Not at all," he assured her. "May I?"

Alexis lifted her hair and turned slightly as Peter fastened the necklace around her neck. "It's absolutely gorgeous," she gushed, admiring it.

Peter touched her shoulder and nodded toward Neil, who had piled a literal mountain of food onto his plate.

"You may want to set up some guardrails for that one." He winked.

Alexis snorted softly. "He looks like he's preparing for hibernation."

Across the room, Santa settled into an armchair by the fireplace. The children gathered at his feet, adults joined behind them in a cozy half-circle. If there was *ever* a man destined to be Santa, it was George Owens: rosy cheeks, wire-rimmed glasses perched at the tip of his nose, a beard like fresh snow, and a belly that truly shook when he laughed—like a bowl full of jelly. Every eye was on him. Every ear attentive as he spoke those first words.

"'Twas the night before Christmas and all through the house—"

The fire crackled and popped behind him, bathing the children's faces in a warm golden glow. They listened attentively, mesmerized. And when he read the last words of the story—"Happy Christmas to all, and to all a good-night!"—the children remained quiet, still caught up in the world of magic and make-believe.

George leaned forward and smiled, his eyes twinkling. "Has everyone been good this year?"

"Yes!" the children shouted out in delight.

"Then I have a little something special for each of you."

The children scooched in closer, their eyes filled with excitement.

George slid a giant red sack tied with a golden bow from behind his chair. He untied the ribbon, his eyes twinkling, looked out at his captive audience of angelic faces, and smiled. "Olivia, if you would?"

Olivia hurried over, shepherding the children into a line in front of Santa—their eyes locked onto the bag of toys.

One by one, each little boy and girl had their moment with Santa. Hugs were given, pictures and videos were taken—memories the parents would cherish forever.

Each child received a hand-wrapped gift with an *Official North Pole* golden seal. Inside each gift was an illustrated copy of *The Night Before Christmas*, a giant candy cane, hot cocoa kit with marshmallows, and a mini LEGO bag.

Soon, the children gathered around Santa again, peppering him with questions about reindeers, elves, and the North Pole.

Alexis joined Neil at the piano and nudged him with a playful smirk. "Come on. Play."

He held out for a minute and then finally acquiesced, revealing a beautiful tenor voice, rivaling Michael Bublé's. Alexis gently swayed her head back and forth as she joined in singing "It's Beginning to Look a Lot Like Christmas." Soon guests gathered around the piano, singing along, swaying with mugs of cider and cocoa.

Michael's phone buzzed in his pocket. He ignored it at first, glancing only long enough to note the unfamiliar number, and let it go to voicemail. He'd just tucked the phone back when it buzzed again—the same number. Annoyed, he cut through the kitchen, and slipped into Olivia's office, closed the door behind him, and answered.

"Check your messages," demanded a raspy voice before Michael could even say hello.

Michael checked his phone. "I don't have any *new* messages."

He could hear an exchange of muffled voices bickering.

"He said he doesn't have any new messages."

"You didn't hit send, you idiot."

Seconds later, Michael's phone dinged.

"Check your messages!" the voice snickered, and then the line went dead.

A wave of dread spread over Michael. He opened the image and gasped.

His beautiful Miata—his pride and joy—was perched atop a twelve-foot mountain of snow in the Walmart parking lot. The beachcombers stood in a circle around the base of the mountain, arms crossed defiantly—their faces smug, triumphant.

Michael shook his head. Bested by a group of octogenarians.

"I guess I'll be Ubering tonight," he muttered.

"Everything okay?" Ellie poked her head into Olivia's office.

"Yeah." Michael turned his phone, showing Ellie the picture of his car, atop Mount Walmart.

Ellie's hand flew to her mouth. She tried valiantly not to laugh. "You knew they were going to get you back."

"You play with fire"—Michael said with a sigh—"you get burned."

Ellie shook her head, amused. "You seem to do that a lot."

"A bit," Michael agreed. He stared at the photo of his car, trying to figure out how he was going to get it down. *Crane, forklift, divine intervention?*

Ellie bumped his shoulder lightly. "I see you had a costume change." She nodded at his sweater. *"Scrumptious—Do Not Leave Unattended."* Her eyes sparkled. "Bold statement."

"Yeah… someone may snatch me away."

"Well we can't have that." Ellie laughed. She slipped her hand into his and tugged gently. "Come on, Neil's playing one of my favorites."

She led him into the kitchen, softly singing along to "Have Yourself a Merry Little Christmas."

But to their surprise, when they rounded the corner, it wasn't Neil singing—it was Gerald, crooning like a 1984 lounge singer.

Mrs. Bartleby stood front and center, one hand on her cane, the other holding up a lighter like she was at a rock concert, the flame flickering dangerously close to her bangs.

"You know," said Michael, feeling the weight of Ellie's head on his shoulder, her hair brushing his jaw. "I don't have a date for New Year's. And last year, I wound up kissing Mrs. Bartleby."

Ellie's head snapped up. "On the lips?"

"On the lips." Michael sighed. "Sadly."

"But she's like… ninety."

"Don't remind me," muttered Michael. "So? Is it a date?"

"I'll have to check my social calendar," Ellie teased. "I'm a heavily sought-after commodity in this…"

"Booming metropolis," Michael finished with a grin.

"Tell you what," Ellie said, swaying with him to Gerald's heartfelt vocals, "I'll think about it." She squeezed his hand, rose up on her toes, and kissed his cheek.

Across the room, Alexis's heart jumped. *Did Ellie just kiss my dad?* Her heart filled with hope.

"What was that?" Michael asked, touching his cheek.

Ellie was silent for a moment, a smile slowly spreading across her face. "I don't know… maybe a hint of what's to come."

Michael was about to reply, when his eyes met Alexis's. She smiled back at him, sending his heart soaring. Perhaps Christmas was magic after all. He swayed along with Ellie, listening to the music, perfectly content just holding her hand.

Merry Christmas!

THANK YOU FOR READING
A ROLE TO DIE FOR!

Thank you so much for reading the third book of *The Coffee House Sleuths.* We hope you enjoyed this cozy mystery. If you think others would enjoy this book, please take a few moments and leave a review on Amazon, Goodreads, Barnes & Noble, Bookbub, etc. You can't imagine how helpful this would be!

If you're in the Christmas mood, check out the first book in *The Coffee House Sleuths: A Christmas Cozy Mystery.* A rogue Santa, a shocking murder, and a small-town full of secrets. Michael and his friends must solve the mystery before Christmas turns deadly. Discover the festive whodunnit in *Sleighed.*

MERRY AND MOODY WITCH COZY MYSTERIES

⇒ Book 1: Potion Commotion

⇒ Book 2: Bittersweet Deceit

Step into a world of magic, mischief, and mystery as two young witches face danger, dark secrets, and brewing trouble. A fast-paced cozy series full of charm, twists, and lovable animal familiars.

OPHELIA P.I.
A SUPERNATURAL MURDER MYSTERY

Love Magical Mysteries? Meet Ophelia Windsor.

From the author of *The Coffee House Sleuths* comes a brand-new series with a darker twist—set in 1950s Illinois and filled with magic, mystery, and a sharp-witted immortal private investigator.

When a factory worker dies under impossible circumstances, Ophelia Windsor—witch, immortal, and private investigator—must untangle a case woven with danger, secrets, and powerful supernatural forces.

THOMAS LOCKHAVEN

In addition to writing adult cozy mysteries, T. Lockhaven also writes children's adventure and mystery novels under the name Thomas Lockhaven. His popular series include:

- ⇒ Ava & Carol Detective Agency – a fast-paced adventure mystery series for young readers.
- ⇒ Ripley Kool and the Investigators – humorous detective adventures featuring curious kids and surprising cases.
- ⇒ Calista Chase: Time Sleuth – time-travel mysteries beginning with Blackbeard's Treasure.
- ⇒ Quest Chasers – a fantasy adventure series full of puzzles, danger, and magic.
- ⇒ The Ghosts of Ian Stanley – a spooky, ongoing mystery series.

To learn about new releases, sign up at twistedkeypublishing.com/tlockhaven

You may also follow T. Lockhaven on Amazon, Goodreads or BookBub.